DISCOVERING AMERICA

The South

ALABAMA • FLORIDA • MISSISSIPPI

By
Thomas G. Aylesworth
Virginia L. Aylesworth

CHELSEA HOUSE PUBLISHERS
New York • Philadelphia

3   5   7   9   8   6   4   2

Library of Congress Cataloging-in-Publication Data

Aylesworth, Thomas G.
    The South: Alabama, Florida, Mississippi
Thomas G. Aylesworth, Virginia L. Aylesworth.
        p. cm.—(Discovering America)
        Includes bibliographical references and index.
        ISBN 0-7910-3240-X.
            0-7910-3421-6 (pbk.)
        1. Southern States—Juvenile literature. 2. Alabama—Juvenile literature. 3. Florida—Juvenile
literature. 4. Mississippi—Juvenile literature. I. Aylesworth, Virginia L. II. Title. III. Series:
Aylesworth, Thomas G. Discovering America.

F209.3.A95   1995   94-40422
975—dc20   CIP
                                                  AC

CONTENTS

ALABAMA

FLORIDA

MISSISSIPPI

Alabama

The great seal of Alabama was adopted in 1939; it is the same design that was used from 1819 until 1868. It is circular and bears a map of the state, showing its boundaries and rivers. Over the map is the word *Alabama*, and under it is inscribed "Great Seal."

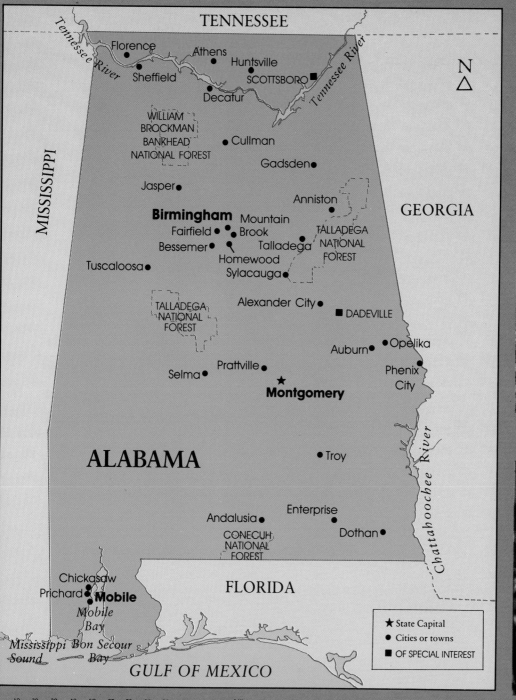

TENNESSEE

Tennessee River

Florence
Athens
Huntsville
Sheffield
SCOTTSBORO
Decatur

Tennessee River

WILLIAM
BROCKMAN
BANKHEAD
NATIONAL FOREST

Cullman
Gadsden

Jasper
Anniston

GEORGIA

Birmingham Mountain
Fairfield Brook
Bessemer Talladega
Homewood
Sylacauga

TALLADEGA
NATIONAL
FOREST

Tuscaloosa

TALLADEGA
NATIONAL
FOREST

Alexander City
■ DADEVILLE

Auburn Opelika

Selma Prattville

Phenix
City

★ **Montgomery**

ALABAMA

Troy

Andalusia
Enterprise

CONECUH
NATIONAL
FOREST

Dothan

Chattahoochee River

FLORIDA

Chickasaw
Prichard **Mobile**

*Mobile
Bay*

*Mississippi Bon Secour
Sound Bay*

GULF OF MEXICO

N
△

MISSISSIPPI

★	State Capital
●	Cities or towns
■	OF SPECIAL INTEREST

0 10 20 30 40 50 60 70 80 90 100   120   Miles
0 10 20 30 40 50 60 70 80 90 100   120   140   160   180   200 Kilometres

Capital: Montgo

ALABAMA
At a Glance

State Flag

State Flower: Camellia
State Bird: Yellowhammer
State Tree: Southern Pine

Size: 51,705 square miles (29th largest)
Population: 4,135,543 (22nd largest)

Major Industries: Pulp and paper, chemicals, electronics, textiles, metals

Major crops: Soybeans, peanuts, corn, hay, wheat, cotton

7

State Flag

The Alabama state flag, officially designated in 1895, has a white background on which is a red cross of St. Andrew, which was the principal feature of the Confederate battle flag.

State Motto

Audemus Jura Nostra Defendere

The motto, which is Latin for "We Dare Defend Our Rights," was adopted in 1923.

A typical tree-lined road in rural Alabama. These trees, a necessity in the summer months, provide relief from the relentless summer heat.

State Name and Nicknames

When Spanish explorers arrived in what was to become Alabama, the first Indians they met were the Alabama Indians, so the Europeans called the wide river there the Alabama River. The territory later took its name from the river. The origin of the name of the Indian tribe is probably Choctaw—*Alba Amo,* meaning "thicket clearers" or "vegetation gatherers."

Alabama has no official nickname, but it is often called the *Yellowhammer State,* after the state bird. Because of the space center in Huntsville, it is also called *The Pioneer Space Capital of the World.* Other nicknames are *Heart of Dixie* and *Cotton State.*

State Flower

In 1927 the goldenrod, *Solidago juncea,* was named the state flower of Alabama. But in 1959, the law designating the goldenrod was repealed and the camellia, *Thea japonica,* was chosen to be the new state flower.

State Fossil

Basilosaurus cetoides, an aquatic dinosaur about 55 feet long, was named the state fossil in 1984.

State Freshwater Fish

In 1975, the largemouth bass, *Micropterus punctulatus,* was designated as the state freshwater fish.

State Horse

The racking horse was named state horse in 1975.

State Mineral

Hematite, an iron ore, has been the state mineral since 1967.

State Tree

In 1949, the southern pine, *Pinus palustris,* was adopted as the state tree. It is also called the longleaf yellow pine, the pitch pine, the hard pine, the heart pine, the turpentine pine, the rosemary pine, the brown pine, the fat pine, the longstraw pine, and the longleaf pitch pine.

State Bird

The yellowhammer, *Colaptes auratus,* was named the state bird in 1927. During the Civil War, Alabama soldiers were called *"yellowhammers"* because of the color of the uniforms of the Huntsville company, which were trimmed in bright yellow. This bird is also called the yellow-shafted flicker.

State Game Bird

In 1980, the wild turkey, *Meleagris gallopavo,* was designated the state game bird of Alabama.

State Dance

Named in 1981, the square dance is the official state dance.

State Nut

The pecan was named state nut in 1982.

State Rock

Marble was designated the state rock in 1969.

State Saltwater Fish

Named in 1955, the tarpon, *Tarpon atlanticus,* is the state saltwater fish.

State Song

"Alabama," with words by Julia S. Tutwiler and music by Edna Goeckel Gussen, was adopted as the state song in 1931.

Population

The population of Alabama in 1992 was 4,135,543, making it the 22nd most populous state. There are 81.5 persons per square mile—68 percent of the population live in metropolitan areas. Approximately 98 percent of Alabamians were born in the United States.

Industries

The principal industries of Alabama are pulp and paper, chemicals, electronics, apparel, textiles, primary metals, lumber and wood, food processing, fabricated metals, and automotive tires. The chief products are electronics, cast-iron and plastic pipe, fabricated steel products, ships, paper products, chemicals. steel, mobile homes, fabrics, and poultry products.

Agriculture

The chief crops of the state are peanuts, cotton, soybeans, hay, corn, wheat, potatoes, pecans, sweet potatoes, and cottonseed. Alabama is also a livestock state; there are estimated to be some 1.8 million cattle, 400,000 hogs and pigs, and 14.8 million chickens on its farms. Pine and hardwoods are harvested, and cement, clay, lime, sand, gravel, and stone are important mineral resources. Commercial fishing brought in $35.6 million in 1992. There are 2.7 million foodsize catfish in Alabama.

Government

The governor of Alabama is elected to a four-year term, as are the lieutenant governor, secretary of state, attorney general, auditor, treasurer, commissioner of agriculture and industries, and eight members of the state board of education. The state legislature, which meets annually, consists of a senate of 35 members and a house of representatives of 105 members each elected to a four-year term. The state's 67 counties elect from 1 to 17 representatives, depending on their populations. The most recent state constitution was adopted in 1901. In addition to its two U.S. senators, Alabama has seven representatives in the U.S. House of Representatives. The state has nine votes in the electoral college.

Sports

Many sporting events on the college and secondary school levels are held all over the state. In 1953, Birmingham won the Little League World Series. Although collegiate basketball is growing in popularity, college football is king in the state. The University of Alabama and Auburn University are perennial national powers, and both schools have appeared in numerous post-season bowl games.

Major Cities

Birmingham (population 284,413). Founded in 1870 and named after the English city, by 1900 Birmingham was being called "The Pittsburgh of the South" because of its steel mills. Today, the city is modern and progressive; it could be termed the heart of the "New South." It is a city of manufacturing, education, and culture.

Places to visit in Birmingham: the Statue of Vulcan, Arlington (1850), the Birmingham Museum of Art, the Alabama Sports Hall of Fame Museum, Discovery Place, Sloss Furnaces National Historic Landmark, the Birmingham Zoo, the Birmingham Botanical Gardens, the Japanese Gardens, the Red Mountain Museum, the Ruffner Mountain Nature Center, and Rickwood Caverns State Park.

Mobile (population 196,278). Founded in 1711, Mobile is Alabama's only port city. It is a city full of Southern grace and Southern enterprise, and Mobile has managed to preserve its heritage in four historical districts: Church Street, DeTonti Square, Oakleigh Garden, and Old Dauphinway, where strollers are shaded on the oak-lined streets.

Places to visit in Mobile: Oakleigh (1830s), Bellingrath Gardens and Home, Richards-DAR House, the Fine Arts Museum of the South, the Exploreum Museum of Discovery, the Cathedral of the Immaculate Conception (1835), the Phoenix Fire Museum, the Carlen House Museum, Fort Conde Mobile Visitor Welcome Center, the Conde-Charlotte Museum House (1824-1825), the Museum of the City of Mobile (1872), the Heustis Medical Museum, the Alabama State Docks, the Battleship USS Alabama Memorial Park, and the Malbis Greek Orthodox Church (1965).

Montgomery (population 187,543). Settled in 1814, this capital city was a great cotton market before the Civil War. Today, the city retains its pride in its history. It was from Montgomery that a telegram was sent ("Fire on Fort Sumter"), starting the Civil War. It was here that the Confederacy was born. And it was here that "Dixie" was set to music by Dan Emmett. Montgomery is a bustling city that retains its Southern charm.

Places to visit in Montgomery: the State Capitol (1851), the First White House of the Confederacy (1835), the Alabama Department of Archives and History, the Governor's Mansion, the Teague House (1848), the Rice-Semple-Haardt House (1855), the Lurleen B. Wallace Museum, the Murphy House

The Montgomery Museum of Fine Arts houses an impressive collection of works by southern artists, as well as an interactive gallery and studio for children.

(1851), the Old North Hull Street District, the Lower Commerce Street Historic District, the Montgomery Museum of Fine Arts, St. John's Episcopal Church (1855), the Dexter Avenue King Memorial Baptist Church (1877), the Montgomery Zoo, the Gayle Space Transit Planetarium, the Jasmine Hill Gardens, Hank Williams' Grave, Maxwell Air Force Base, and Fort Toulouse/Jackson Park National Historic Landmark.

Places to Visit

The National Park Service maintains eight areas in the state of Alabama: part of the Natchez Trace Parkway, Horseshoe Bend National Military Park, Russell Cave National Monument, Tuskegee Institute National Historic Site, Bankhead National Forest, Conecuh National Forest, Talladega National Forest, and Tuskegee National Forest. In addition, there are 22 state recreational areas.

Anniston: Dr. J. C. Francies Medical Museum and Apothecary. Built in 1850, this is a former doctor's office.

Clanton: Confederate Memorial Park. This Confederate cemetery also contains a museum of Civil War momentos.

Cullman: Ave Maria Grotto. Some 150 miniaturized replicas of famous churches and shrines are located on four acres of landscaped hillside.

Dauphin Island: Fort Gaines. Built in the 1850s, this Civil War fort contains a museum.

Decatur: Old Decatur and Albany Historic Districts. This neighborhood contains three pre-Civil War and 194 Victorian buildings.

Demopolis: Bluff Hall. Built in 1832, this is a restored Greek Revival mansion.

Dothan: Opera House. This 590-seat theater was built in 1915.

Eufaula: Seth Lore and Irwinton Historic District. There are 582 registered landmark buildings in this district.

Florence: W. C. Handy Home and Museum. This is the restored birthplace of the man who wrote "St. Louis Blues."

Fort Payne: Sequoyah Caverns and Campgrounds. Surrounding this fascinating cave are fields where deer and buffalo live.

Huntsville: The Space and Rocket Center. Exhibits of capsules and space shuttle objects, films, and tours of NASA activities.

Ozark: Holman Mansion. Built in 1912, this Greek Revival home has beautiful stained glass and handpainted stenciling on the walls.

Phenix City: Old Russell County Courthouse. This, the third-oldest courthouse in the state, was built in 1868.

Russellville: Dismals. This wilderness area contains trees more than 100 feet high,

The dramatic lighting in Sequoyah Caverns create the appearance of an underground palace.

natural bridges, and waterfalls.

Selma: Old Town Historic District. This district contains some 600 old buildings.

Talladega: International Motorsports Hall of Fame. The hall contains memorabilia and displays of motor sports.

Troy: Pike Pioneer Museum. Reconstructed buildings recreate nineteenth-century life here.

Tuscaloosa: Strickland House. Built in 1820, this is the oldest wooden house in the county.

Tuscumbia: Ivy Green. Built in 1820, this was the birthplace and early home of Helen Keller.

Tuskegee: George Washington Carver Museum. This includes exhibits and the original laboratory of the scientific genius.

Events

There are many events and organizations that schedule activities of various kinds in the state of Alabama. Here are some of them:

Sports: Alabama Deep-Sea Fishing Rodeo (Dauphin Island); Racking Horse World Celebration (Decatur); Wiregrass Quarter Horse Circuit Show (Dothan); International Billfishing Tournament (Gulf Shores); Senior Bowl Football Game (Mobile); greyhound racing at Mobile Greyhound Park (Mobile); Southern Livestock Exposition and Rodeo (Montgomery); stock and sports car races at the Alabama International Motor Speedway (Talladega); greyhound racing at Greenetrack (Tuscaloosa).

Arts and Crafts: Homespun (Athens); Dogwood Festival (Birmingham); Festival of the Arts (Birmingham); Southern Wildlife Festival (Decatur); Azalea Dogwood Festival (Dothan); Mentone Crafts Festival in Brow City Park (Fort Payne); Folklife Festival (Huntsville); Azalea Trail Festival (Mobile).

Music: Musical Explosion (Athens); Tennessee Valley Old Time Fiddlers Convention (Athens); Alabama Symphony Orchestra (Birmingham);

Decatur Chamber Orchestra (Decatur); W. C. Handy Music Festival (Florence); June Jam (Fort Payne); Huntsville Symphony (Huntsville); Panoply of the Arts Festival (Huntsville); Country Jam (Ozark); Cahawba Day (Selma).

Entertainment: Mayfest (Atmore); Homecoming and Powwow (Atmore); State Fair (Birmingham); Alabama Jubilee (Decatur); Spirit of America Festival (Decatur); Joe Wheeler Civil War Reenactment (Decatur); Christmas on the River (Demopolis); Alabama Air Fair (Dothan); National Peanut Festival (Dothan); Indian Summer Days (Eufaula); DeKalb County VFW Agricultural Fair (Fort Payne); Mardi Gras Celebration (Gulf Shores); Sea Oats Jazz and Arts Festival (Gulf Shores); National Shrimp Festival (Gulf Shores); Northeast Alabama State Fair (Huntsville); Mardi Gras (Mobile); Blessing of the Shrimp Fleet (Mobile); Greater Gulf State Fair (Mobile); Jubilee (Montgomery); South Alabama Fair (Montgomery); Russell County Courthouse Fair (Phenix City); Central Alabama Fair (Selma); Tale Telling Festival (Selma); Helen Keller Festival (Sheffield).

Tours: Christmas Heritage Tour (Bessemer); Plantation Homes Tour (Birmingham);

Christmas in Canebrake (Demopolis); Eufaula Pilgrimage (Eufaula); Heritage Tour (Florence); Cotton Harvest (Huntsville); Historic Mobile Tours (Mobile); Black Heritage Tour (Selma); Historic Selma Pilgrimage (Selma); Tuscaloosa Heritage Week (Tuscaloosa).

Theater: Princess Theater (Decatur); Alabama Shakespeare Festival (Montgomery); "The Miracle Worker" (Tuscumbia).

The Space Orientation Center in Huntsville displays rockets and other equipment used in U.S. space programs.

The Land and the Climate

Although the highest spot in Alabama is Cheaha Mountain, at 2,407 feet, most of the state is less than 500 feet above sea level. Its surface rises gradually toward the northeast. Alabama has six main land regions: the East Gulf Coastal Plain, the Black Belt, the Piedmont, the Appalachian Ridge and Valley Region, the Cumberland Plateau, and the Interior Low Plateau.

A farmer harvests peanuts on a large plantation. Peanuts have recently become one of Alabama's leading crops, and the trend in the state's farming industry has been toward fewer and larger farms.

The East Gulf Coastal Plain covers most of the southern two-thirds of the state. Many farms throughout the area produce cotton, peanuts, fruit, dairy products, hogs, and beef cattle. The plain has several sections. The Mobile River Delta, in the southwest, is a region of low, swampy land. In the southeast is the Wiregrass area, named for the tough grass that used to grow in the pine forests there—it is now an important farming region. The northern part of the plain is also called the Central Pine Belt because of the forests on its low hills.

The Black Belt is a strip of fertile prairie between the northern and southern parts of the East Gulf Coastal Plain. Named for the black clay soils found there, it once contained many cotton plantations and now has numerous livestock farms which flourish on its good pastureland.

The Piedmont, in east-central Alabama, is characterized by low hills and sandy valleys. Most of the area is forested, but there are deposits of coal, iron ore, limestone, and marble. These natural resources, plus the hydroelectric power from projects on the Coosa and Tallapoosa Rivers, make the Piedmont an important manufacturing area.

The Appalachian Ridge and Valley Region contains sandstone ridges and fertile valleys beneath which are limestone deposits. It is located between the Piedmont and the Cumberland Plateau to the north. Here coal and iron ore, in addition to the limestone, provide the three basic materials necessary for making iron and steel. Birmingham is a center for the manufacture of these products.

The Cumberland Plateau is northwest of the Appalachian Ridge and Valley Region, and is also called the Appalachian Plateau. It is a land of flat fields and gradual slopes that rise to a height of about 1,800 feet in the northeast. There were few farms here until the 1880s, because the soil would not support crops. But with the development of

Noccalula Falls, in Gadsden, is part of the northeastern Appalachian Ridge and Valley Region. This area is rich in mineral resources and provides the state with much of the raw material needed for manufacturing iron and steel.

Birmingham, in the foothills of the Appalachian mountain chain, is one of the state's most important industrial centers. With a population of approximately 265,000, it is Alabama's largest city.

commercial fertilizers, farmers began to grow hogs, poultry, cotton, hay, potatoes, and vegetables in this region.

The Interior Low Plateau is located in the northwestern part of Alabama, much of it in the Tennessee River Valley. Here there are corn, cotton, and hay farms. Hydroelectric power from the rivers also encourages manufacturing in the region.

Alabama has a 53-mile coastline on the Gulf of Mexico in the southwest section of the state; this shoreline would total 607 miles if all the bays and inlets were measured. Mobile Bay is the chief harbor area. Almost every section of Alabama contains navigable rivers, and Mobile River and its tributaries form the state's most important river system. Other important rivers are the Alabama, the Tombigbee, the Chattahoochee, and the Tennessee. The state has no large natural lakes, but dams have created several man-made lakes. The largest is Lake Guntersville, which has an area of 110 square miles.

Alabama's southern location in the North American Continent gives it a mild climate throughout the year. In January, temperatures rarely fall below 43 degrees Fahrenheit, and in July they average 82 degrees F. Snowfall is rare, with rain varying from 53 inches annually in the north to 68 inches along the coast.

Alabama tourists enjoy the leisurely pace and old-fashioned charm of a riverboat cruise. Almost every section of Alabama contains navigable rivers, with the Mobile River and its tributaries forming the state's most important river system.

The History

Some 8,000 years ago, what would become Alabama was the home of many cliff-dwelling Indians. Archaeological digs in Russell Cave in northeastern Jackson County have uncovered evidence of their daily lives, including tools, weapons, and food preparation. Much later came the Cherokee, Creek, Choctaw, and Chickasaw. These Indians were part of what were called the Civilized Tribes, with a sophisticated culture that included permanent dwellings, religious rites, farming, hunting and fishing.

The first white man to arrive in the region was probably Alonzo Álvarez de Piñeda, a Spanish explorer who sailed into Mobile Bay in 1519. Another Spaniard, Pánfilo de Narváez, explored the coastal waters of Alabama. One member of his expedition was Cabeza de Vaca, the first European to cross North America. Another Spanish expedition, led by Hernando de Soto, came into the territory from the northeast in 1540. De Soto was the first white man to explore the interior region and to fight the native peoples on a large scale. At Mabila, in what is now Clarke County, he defeated Chief Tuskalusa and his Choctaws and burned their village. This pattern would persist until all the Five Civilized Tribes had been driven out of their homeland several centuries later.

Tristán de Luna, another Spaniard, based in Mexico, looked for gold in Alabama in 1559, setting up small settlements on Mobile Bay and at the site where Claiborne is now located. But in 1561 he was ordered back to Mexico and the outposts were abandoned.

The French arrived in 1702 and were the first white men to settle in the area for any length of time. Two French-Canadian brothers, Pierre and Jean Baptiste Le Moyne, built Fort Louis on the Mobile River in that year. Because of flooding, however, the colony moved 27 miles south, to the site of present-day Mobile, in 1711. This became the first permanent settlement in Alabama. Here the French built a new

The French built Fort Condé (originally named Fort Louis) in 1717. Located in what is now Mobile, it helped the French establish their presence in the South and served as a military headquarters until 1763. Parts of the fort have been restored since its destruction more than 150 years ago, and guides now demonstrate facsimiles of 18th-century cannons and muskets for visitors.

Fort Louis, changing its name to Fort Condé in 1720. (When the British took it over in 1763, it was renamed Fort Charlotte.) While the French were establishing a presence in the south, the British were settling in the north, having moved in from Tennessee.

It was in 1763 that the French turned over their territories in North America to the British—a result of the Treaty of Paris, which ended the long French and Indian Wars. The Mobile area became part of the territory of West Florida, and the northern area was joined to the Illinois country. The Illinois region was set aside as a hunting ground for the Indians, but white settlers continued to move into it. As a result, during the American Revolution, many Indian tribes sided with the British, fighting the rebellious colonists who were moving west.

In 1864 Fort Morgan, on Mobile Point, became one of the last Confederate forts to fall to Union forces.

In 1779 Spain began to support the Americans in the War for Independence, and the following year the Spaniard Bernardo Gálvez captured Mobile from the British. After the British had deeded Mobile to the Spanish in the Treaty of Paris of 1783, the United States negotiated the Treaty of San Lorenzo with Spain, which gave all of Alabama except the Mobile area to the Americans. But during the War of 1812 against the English, the Americans seized Mobile, and their flag flew over all of Alabama.

In 1813 several hundred settlers were massacred at Fort Mims, near Tensaw, by Creek Indians. The next year, American troops under General Andrew Jackson defeated the Creek in the Battle of Horseshoe Bend. William Weatherford (Red Eagle), a Creek chief of mixed Indian and American parentage, was the loser in this hopeless battle, and all Creek lands were ceded to the United States.

The Alabama Territory was organized in 1817, with Saint Stephens, a town on the Tombigbee River, as its capital. A state constitution was written in 1819, and on December 14 of that year Alabama became the 22nd state to enter the Union. Huntsville served as the new state capital for a year, and William Wyatt Bibb became the first governor. In 1820 Cahaba was designated the capital, but floods from the Alabama River destroyed much of the town, and the seat of state government moved to Tuscaloosa in 1826. Montgomery became the permanent capital 20 years later. Meanwhile, almost all the Alabama Indian tribes had been forcibly relocated west of the Mississippi River.

Horseshoe Bend, near Dadeville, is the site of General Andrew Jackson's victory over the Creek Indians on March 27, 1814. This final defeat of the Creek accelerated the removal of Indian tribes from Alabama and, consequently, helped American pioneers seize Indian lands for settlement.

At left:
Jefferson Davis was chosen provisional president of the Confederacy in February 1861. The office was created soon after Alabama joined Georgia, Florida, Louisiana, Mississippi, South Carolina, and Texas in forming the Confederate States of America.

Below:
The First White House of the Confederacy was home to President and Mrs. Jefferson Davis while Montgomery served as the capital of the Confederate States of America. On May 21, 1861, the seat of government was moved to Richmond, Virginia.

Benjamin Sterling Turner, Alabama's first black congressman, was born a slave in North Carolina. As a child in Alabama, he secretly taught himself to read and became an invaluable assistant to Dr. James T. Gee, owner of the St. James, Selma's finest antebellum hotel. After the Civil War, Turner set up his own livery stable and quickly became the richest black in Dallas County. In 1868 he was elected county tax collector and Selma city councilman. Two years later, with overwhelming support from his home county, he won election to Congress and began a fight for civil rights in the House of Representatives.

After Abraham Lincoln was elected president, the southern states, fearing that slavery would be outlawed, began to secede, or withdraw, from the Union. Alabama seceded on January 11, 1861, renaming itself the Republic of Alabama. A convention was set up in Montgomery to which the other southern states sent delegates. This convention formed the Confederate States of America, and Montgomery was named as the capital. Confederate President Jefferson Davis was inaugurated there. In May, 1861, the capital was moved to Richmond, Virginia, but Montgomery is still known as the Cradle of the Confederacy.

Union Admiral David G. Farragut won the Battle of Mobile Bay—the most important Civil War battle fought in Alabama—in 1864. Union troops made several raids into the state during the war, the largest of which was General James H. Wilson's cavalry campaign of 1865. But Alabama suffered less destruction during the war than most of the Confederate States. During Reconstruction, the nine-year period of military occupation that followed the war, dishonest government and hostile factions reduced the state to disorder and indebtedness. Alabama was readmitted to the Union in 1868, but reform of state government came only in 1875, after adoption of a new constitution.

Prosperity began to return with the building of the railroads in the 1870s and creation of the iron and steel manufacturing industries, which had become Alabama's most important by 1890. Lumber and textiles became major sources of revenue. After the United States entered World War I in 1917, shipbuilding began to boom in Mobile, and Alabama farmers supplied vast quantities of cotton and food to the war effort.

During the Great Depression of the 1930s, more than 60 Alabama banks failed, and many farmers went bankrupt. Employment increased in 1933, when the Federal Government formed the Tennessee Valley Authority (TVA) to build major flood-control and hydroelectric projects on the Tennessee River. Muscle Shoals was the headquarters for the huge undertaking, which brought new industry into the state.

During World War II (1941–45), agriculture and industrial production expanded again, as Alabama contributed food, iron, steel, munitions, ships, and textiles to the war effort. Thousands of troops were trained at Fort McClellan and Camp Rucker. Maxwell Field at Montgomery was one of the largest aviation warfare schools in the world.

After the war, Redstone Arsenal at Huntsville, which had been established in 1941, supported the work of international scientists who developed rockets, space satellites, and other technological breakthroughs. Civil rights concerns flared in the 1950s, as Dr. Martin Luther King, Jr., led protests in Montgomery in 1955 and 1956. Rosa Parks, a black Alabamian, refused to give her seat to a white man on a Montgomery City Bus. Her subsequent arrest led to a city bus boycott organized by E.D. Nixon and later by Dr. King. The boycott lasted one year before seating on city buses was integrated. A 1963 bombing attack on a black church that killed four children prompted many white citizens to action and to support black citizens. In 1965, a five-day Freedom March from Selma to Montgomery culminated in 30,000 civil rights demonstrators protesting at the state capitol. This march helped to win passage of the national Voting Rights Act. Throughout the 1960s and 1970s and to the present day, Alabama continues to confront problems of race and segregation, both voluntary and involuntary. Alabama has changed significantly during its evolution from the capital of the confederacy to the herald of the Space Age, but this vigorous state retains its traditional charm.

The USS *Alabama* is permanently berthed in Mobile Bay. The 35,000-ton battleship was launched in 1942 and earned battle stars in all the major Pacific engagements of World War II. In 1965 it was designated a state shrine honoring the courage of Alabamians who served in World War II and the Korean conflict.

Education

The Alabama Public School System was established in 1854, but it was not actively implemented until 1900. Alabama schools were segregated until 1963 in response to the 1954 U.S. Supreme Court decision

A portrait of Helen Adams Keller, American writer and lecturer, born in Tuscumbia. Blind and deaf from infancy, Keller learned from a private teacher, Anne Sullivan, to read, write, and communicate by touch. Later, she learned to speak. In addition to furthering the work of the American Foundation for the Blind, Helen Keller served as a profound inspiration for people all over the world. The much-acclaimed Broadway play and a subsequent movie, *The Miracle Worker*, are based on her life and that of Anne Sullivan.

which made segregation unconstitutional. In 1956, Autherine Lucy became the first black to enroll at the previously all-white school, The University of Alabama. In June 1963, Governor George Wallace twice blocked the admission of blacks to the university; but President John F. Kennedy sent the Alabama National Guard both times to stop this action, and the students were admitted. In September 1963 Wallace barred black pupils from attending Alabama public schools and Kennedy once again ordered the Alabama National Guard to active duty to enforce federal court orders for integrated schools. For the first time, Negro students began attending previously all-white schools. In 1968, 86 percent of black students attended all black schools. In

1981, 24 percent of black students attended all black schools, primarily by choice, and 40 percent of black students attended schools where the majority of pupils were white.

The People

About 60 percent of the people in the state of Alabama live in metropolitan areas. Just under 99 percent of Alabama residents were born in the United States. The largest religious groups are the Baptists and the Methodists. Other prominent denominations in Alabama include the Disciples of Christ, Episcopalians, Jews, Lutherans, Presbyterians, and Roman Catholics.

In Tuskegee, Booker Taliaferro Washington founded the Tuskegee Institute in 1881. In an effort to gain equal rights and opportunities for blacks in the South, the school trained students to be farmers, mechanics, teachers, and tradesmen. Washington served as principal of the Institute until his death in 1915.

Famous People

Many famous people were born in the state of Alabama. Here are a few:

Hank Aaron b. 1934, Mobile. Hall of Fame baseball player

Mel Allen b. 1913, Birmingham. Baseball announcer

Tallulah Bankhead 1903-1968, Huntsville. Award-

Hank Aaron holds the major-league record for the most career home runs (755) and runs batted in (2,297); he played 23 seasons in the majors.

winning stage and film actress

William Brockman Bankhead 1874-1940, Moscow. Speaker of the U.S. House of Representatives

Hugo Black 1886-1971, Harlan. Supreme Court justice

Lyman Bostock 1950-1978, Birmingham. Baseball player

Nell Carter b. 1948, Birmingham. Singer, Tony Award–winning actress in theater, television, and film: *Hair*

Nat "King" Cole 1917-1965, Montgomery. Pop singer

Angela Davis b. 1944, Birmingham. Black militant

John Drew b. 1954, Vredenburgh. Basketball player

Louise Fletcher b. 1936, Birmingham. Academy Award-winning actress: *One Flew Over the Cuckoo's Nest*

George Foster b. 1948, Tuscaloosa. Baseball player

Tallulah Bankhead was well known for her intelligence, beauty, and exuberance. To many she symbolized the best of the "roaring twenties."

Kenneth Gibson b. 1932, Enterprise. First black mayor of Newark, New Jersey

William C. Gorgas 1854-1920, near Mobile. Physician and conqueror of malaria and yellow fever

Lionel Hampton b. 1913, Birmingham. Jazz vibraphonist

W. C. Handy 1873-1958, Florence. Blues composer

Bo Jackson b. 1962, Bessemer. Football and baseball player

Kate Jackson b. 1948, Birmingham. TV actress: *The Rookies, Charlie's Angels*

Helen Keller 1880-1968, Tuscumbia. Deaf and blind woman who became an example of achievement

Coretta Scott King b. 1927, Marion. Civil rights leader and widow of Dr. Martin Luther King, Jr.

Harper Lee b. 1926, Monroeville. Pulitzer Prize-winning novelist: *To Kill A Mockingbird*

Joe Louis 1914-1981, Lexington. Heavyweight boxing champion

Willie Mays b. 1931, Westfield. Hall of Fame baseball player

Willie McCovey b.1938, Mobile. Hall of Fame baseball player

Alexander McGillivray 1759-1793, near Montgomery. Creek Indian leader who fought the U.S. government to return Indian lands

John Hunt Morgan 1825-1864, Huntsville. Confederate general who lead the Morgan Raiders during the Civil War

Jim Nabors b. 1933, Sylacauga. TV actor and singer: *The Andy Griffith Show; Gomer Pyle, U.S.M.C.*

Edgar Daniel Nixon 1899-1987, location unknown. Civil rights activist who helped organize the first successful black labor union

Jesse Owens 1913-1980, Danville. Olympic gold-medal winner in track and field

Satchel Paige 1906-1982, Mobile. Hall of Fame baseball pitcher

Rosa Louise Parks b. 1913, Tuskegee. Civil rights activist

Claude Pepper 1900-1989, Dudleyville. Senator, congressman, and champion of the aged

Walker Percy b. 1916, Birmingham. Novelist: *The Last Gentleman, Love in the Ruins*

Wilson Pickett b. 1941, Prattville. Rhythm-and blues-singer

Lionel Richie b. 1950, Tuskegee. Singer, both solo and with the Commodores; songwriter; producer

Holland "Howlin' Mad" Smith 1882-1967, Seale. World War II Marine Corps general

Pine Top Smith 1904-1929, Troy. Boogie-woogie pianist

Ken Stabler b. 1945, Foley. Football quarterback

Bart Starr b. 1934, Montgomery. Hall of Fame football quarterback

Don Sutton b. 1945, Clio. Baseball pitcher

John H. Vincent 1832-1920, Tuscaloosa. Methodist bishop and founder of the Chautauqua movement

Toni Tenille b. 1943, Montgomery. Pop-rock singer of The Captain and Tenille

Julia Strudwick Tutwiler
1841-1916, location
unknown. Social reformer
and writer who's poem
''Alabama'' was adopted as
the state song in 1931

Dinah Washington 1924-
1963, Tuscaloosa. Blues
singer

Hank Williams 1923-1953,
Georgiana. Country-and-
western singer

Tammy Wynette b. 1942, Red
Bay. Country-and-western
singer

Early Wynn b. 1920,
Hartford. Hall of Fame
baseball pitcher

Colleges and Universities
There are many colleges and

universities in Alabama. Here
are the more prominent, with
their locations, dates of
founding, and enrollments.

*Alabama Agricultural and
Mechanical University*,
Normal, 1873, 5,069.

Alabama State University,
Montgomery, 1874, 5,800.

Auburn University, Auburn,
1856, 21,551.

Birmingham-Southern College,
Birmingham, 1856, 1,763.

Huntingdon College,
Montgomery, 1854, 760.

Jacksonville State University,
Jacksonville, 1883, 8,022.

Oakwood College, Huntsville,
1896, 1,225.

Livingston University,
Livingston, 1840, 1,977.

Samford University,
Birmingham, 1841, 4,248.

Spring Hill College, Mobile,
1830, 1,273.

Troy State University, Troy,
1887, 4,750.

Tuskegee Institute, Tuskegee,
1881, 3,598.

University of Alabama, at
Tuscaloosa, 1831, 18,784; at
Birmingham, 1969, 16,658, at
Huntsville, 1950, 8,026.

**Where to Get More
Information**
Alabama State Chamber of
Commerce
468 S. Perry St., P.O. Box 76
Montgomery, Alabama 36195
or call, 1-800-ALABAMA

Florida

The state seal of Florida, adopted in 1868 and revised in 1985, is circular. As mandated by the state legislature, the design elements of the seal are the sun, a sabal palmetto tree, a steamboat, and a female Indian. Around the circle is written "Great Seal of the State of Florida" and "In God We Trust."

FLORIDA
At a Glance

Capital: Tallahassee

State Flower: Orange Blossom

State Bird: Mockingbird

Major Industries: Services, trade, manufacturing, tourism

Major Crops: Citrus fruits, vegetables, cattle, hogs

ALABAMA

Pensacola

Panama City

Tallahas:

APALACH
NATION
FOREST

★ State Capital
● Cities or towns
■ OF SPECIAL INTEREST

GEORGIA

OSCEOLA NATIONAL FOREST

Jacksonville

ATLANTIC OCEAN

FLORIDA

SAINT AUGUSTINE

Gainesville

OCALA NATIONAL FOREST

Daytona Beach

Titusville

Orlando

Merritt Island
Melbourne
COCOA BEACH

Lakeland
Clearwater
Tampa
LAKE WALES
WINTER HAVEN

Vero Beach

Saint Petersburg

Fort Pierce

Sarasota

West Palm Beach

Fort Myers

LOXAHATCHEE NATIONAL WILDLIFE REFUGE

GULF OF MEXICO

Fort Lauderdale

Miami

EVERGLADES NATIONAL PARK

N

Ponce de Leon Bay

Florida Bay

KEY LARGO

Florida Keys

Key West

Straits of Florida

| 20 | 40 | 60 | 80 | 100 | 120 | 140 | 160 | 180 | 200 | Miles |
| 40 | 60 | 80 | 100 | 120 | 140 | 160 | 180 | 200 | 250 | 300 | Kilometres |

State Flag

State Motto: In God We Trust
State Tree: Sabal Palmetto Palm
Nickname: Sunshine State
State Song: "Swanee River"

Size: 58,664 square miles (22nd largest)
Population: 13,487,621 (4th largest)

State Flag

The state flag of Florida has a white background with two diagonal red stripes, representing the bars on the Confederate flag. In the center is the state seal. The flag was adopted in 1899.

A sweeping look at Miami Beach. Miami Beach is in fact an island connected to the city of Miami by bridges and causeways.

State Name and Nicknames

Florida was discovered on Easter Sunday in 1513 by the Spanish explorer Ponce de León. He therefore named it for the Spanish Easter Feast of Flowers—Pascua Florida.

Florida is most often called the *Sunshine State,* but it is also referred to as the *Alligator State,* the *Everglades State,* and the *Southernmost State.* Because of the importance of the citrus industry, it is sometimes called the *Orange State.*

State Flower

In 1909, the orange blossom, from the tree of the family *Rutaceae,* was named the state flower.

State Tree

Sabal palmetto, the sabal palmetto palm, was adopted as the state tree in 1953. It is also called the cabbage palm, the cabbage palmetto, the palmetto, the tree palmetto, and Bank's palmetto.

State Bird

The mockingbird, *Mimus polyglottos,* named state bird in 1927, was the winner of a statewide vote.

State Air Fair

The Central Florida Air Fair was adopted as the state air fair in 1976.

State Animal

The Florida panther, *Felis concolor,* was selected as state animal in 1982.

State Beverage

In 1967, orange juice from the species *Citrus sinensis* and its hybrids was chosen as the state beverage.

State Festival

Named in 1980 as state festival was "Calle Ocho — Open House 8," a festival held annually in Dade County.

State Freshwater Fish

The Florida largemouth bass, *Micropterus salmoides floridanus,* was adopted as state freshwater fish in 1975.

This house, located in St. Augustine, is the nation's oldest and it was built in the late 16th century. This is one of the many sights that tourists can attend when they visit Florida.

State Gem

The moonstone, chosen in 1970, is the state gem.

State Litter Control Symbol

The litter control trademark of the Florida Federation of Garden Clubs, Inc., "Glenn Glitter," was adopted in 1978.

State Marine Mammal

In 1975, the manatee,

Trichechus latirostris, also called the sea cow, was named the state marine mammal in 1975.

State Pageant

"Indian River," presented annually in Brevard County, was adopted as state pageant in 1979.

State Play

The historical pageant "Cross and Sword," presented annually in St.

Augustine, was chosen as state play in 1973.

State Saltwater Fish

The Atlantic sailfish, *Istiophorus platypterus,* was designated as state saltwater fish in 1975.

State Saltwater Mammal

The porpoise, *Delphinus delphis,* was named the state saltwater mammal in 1975.

The Calle Ocho festival, held in Little Havana, celebrates the region's Cuban heritage.

State Shell

The shell of *Pleuroploca gigantea,* the horse conch or giant band shell, was adopted as state shell in 1969.

State Stone

Agatized coral was named the state stone in 1979.

State Song

In 1935, Stephen Foster's "Old Folks at Home," also known as "Swanee River," was named the state song.

Population

The population of Florida in 1992 was 13,487,621, making it the fourth most populous state. There are 249.8 people per square mile—89 percent of the population live in metropolitan areas. According to the 1990 Census, 9 of the 10 fastest growing metropolitan areas between 1980 and 1990 were in Florida. Punta Gorda, Florida, had the highest percentage change in population with an 89.8 percent increase between 1980 and 1990. In 1992 Punta Gorda had a population of

110,975. About 87 percent of all Floridians were born in the United States. The largest groups of people born in foreign countries have come from Cuba, Canada, England, Germany, and Russia.

Visitors feed the alligators at Homosassa Springs in central western Florida. Tourism is important to the local economy here, as it is throughout the state.

Industries

The principal industries of the state of Florida are services, trade, manufacturing, and tourism. Florida has the highest percentage of people employed in the trade and wholesale and retail sectors with 22 percent of its employees in the trade sector and 24.2 percent of employees in the wholesale and retail sectors. In 1990, out-of-state visitors spent $26.6 billion. The chief manufactured products are electric and electronic equipment, transportation equipment, food, printing and publishing, and machinery.

Agriculture

The chief crops of the state are citrus fruits, vegetables, potatoes, melons, strawberries, and sugar cane. Florida is also a livestock state. There are estimated to be some 1.97 million cattle, 150,000 hogs and pigs, 7,360 sheep, and 13.5 million chickens on its farms. Pine,

cypress, and cedar are harvested, and cement, phosphate rock, and crushed stone are important mineral resources. Commercial fishing earned $154.9 million in 1992.

Government

The governor of Florida serves a four-year term, as do the attorney general, the commissioner of agriculture, the comptroller, the secretary of state, the commissioner of education, and the treasurer. The state legislature, which meets annually, consists of a 40-member senate and a 120-member house of representatives. Senators serve four-year terms, and representatives serve two-year terms. All legislators are elected by district. The most recent state constitution was adopted in 1968. In addition to its two U.S. senators, Florida has 23 representatives in the United States House of Representatives. The state has 25 votes in the electoral college.

Sports

Many sporting events on the collegiate and secondary school levels are played all over the state. Florida State University, the University of Florida, and the University of Miami are perennial football powers. All three schools have appeared in numerous post-season bowl games. There are 28 professional sports teams in Florida. The Tampa Bay Lightning of the National Hockey League plays in Florida, the Miami Dolphins of the National Football League play in Joe Robbie Stadium, the Tampa Bay Buccaneers play in Tampa Stadium, and the Jaguars play in Jacksonville. The Miami Heat and the Orlando Magic of the National Basketball Association play in Florida. Eighteen major league baseball teams have their spring training camps in Florida and play exhibition games in the early spring. The major-league Marlins play the regular season in Miami.

Major Cities

Jacksonville (population 635,230). Settled by the British in 1822, it was first known as Cowford. But when Florida became part of the United States, the town was renamed to honor Andrew Jackson. After the Seminole Wars, the city became a prosperous harbor town. During the Civil War, Jacksonville was occupied four times by the Union troops. After the war, it became a popular winter resort. Today, it is a city of skyscrapers and a major business center.

Places to visit in Jacksonville: the Jacksonville Zoological Park, the Cummer Gallery of Art, the Museum of Science and History, the Jacksonville Art Museum, the Kingsley Plantation State Historic Site, and Little Talbot Island State Park.

Miami (population 358,648). Settled in 1870, Miami was only a remote tropical village until 1896, when the East Coast Railway arrived. In the 1920s, the land boom brought 25,000 real estate salesmen to town. Today, it is home to numerous manufacturing companies, banks, hotels and motels, restaurants, churches and synagogues, and hospitals.

Places to visit in Miami: the Vizcaya Museum and Gardens, the Museum of Science and Space Transit Planetarium, the Historical Museum of South Florida, the Cloisters of the Monastery of St. Bernard de Clairvaux, the Japanese Garden, the Metrozoo, the Parrot Jungle and Gardens, Seaquarium, the Planet Ocean, the Gold Coast Railroad, the Monkey Jungle, the Bayside Marketplace, Little Havana, Lummus Park, the Miccosukee Indian Village, and the Wilderness Experiences/Everglades Institute.

St. Petersburg (population 240,318). Founded in 1876, the fourth most populous city in the state is a favorite with vacationers and retirees. It is also a center of the aerospace and appliance industries.

Places to visit in St. Petersburg: the St. Petersburg Historical Museum, the Hass Museum, the Salvador Dali Museum, the Museum of Fine Arts, the Science Center of Pinellas Country, Great Explorations, the Planetarium, Florida's Sunken Gardens, and The Pier.

Tallahassee (population 124,773). Founded in 1824, the capital city retains both the grace of the old plantation days and its rustic pioneer past. It is also a center of lumber and wood production, printing, publishing, and food production.

Places to visit in Tallahassee: the Historic Old Capitol-

The Villa Vizcaya, now a museum, was built between 1914 and 1922 by James Deering, an heir to the International Harvester fortune. It cost an astonishing 15 million dollars.

The style known as Miami Art Deco was developed in the late 1930s on the south end of Miami Beach. More than 800 of these buildings have been preserved in Art Deco Historic District.

State Building, the State Capitol, the Governor's Mansion (1957), the First Presbyterian Church (1832), the Tallahassee Junior Museum, the LeMoyne Art Foundation, The Columns (1830), the Museum of Florida History, the Alfred B. Maclay State Gardens and the San Marcos de Apalache State Museum.

Tampa (population 280,015). Settled in 1823, it traces its history back to Fort Brooke, which was built to oversee the Seminole Indians. During the Civil War, it was the subject of raids and began to decline as a business center. It grew again with the building of the South Florida Railroad. Tampa was a major staging area in the Spanish-American War. Today, it is a major port and the business hub of the west coast of Florida.

Places to visit in Tampa: Ybor City, the Ybor City State Museum, Busch Gardens— "The Dark Continent," the Tampa Museum of Art, the Hillsborough County Historical Commission Museum, the Museum of Science and Industry, Adventure Island, Lowry Park, and the Waterfront.

Places to Visit

The National Park Service maintains 12 areas in the state of Florida: Castillo de San Marcos National Monument, Fort Jefferson National

A scenic look at the sunrise over Tallahassee. The city was the only Confederate capital east of the Mississippi that was not captured by Union troops during the Civil War.

Monument, Fort Matanzas National Monument, De Soto National Memorial, Fort Caroline National Memorial, Biscayne National Park, Everglades National Park, part of the Gulf Islands National Seashore, Cape Canaveral National Seashore, Apalachicola National Forest, Ocala National Forest, and Osceola National Forest. In addition, there are 59 state recreation areas.

Bradenton: Manatee Village Historical Park. The renovated buildings open for exhibit include the Stephens House, an excellent example of a rural Florida farmhouse.

Brooksville: Weeki Wachee Spring. An underwater ballet, comedy, tableaus, and acrobatics can be seen in the extraordinary underground auditorium.

Clearwater: Clearwater Marine Science Center and

Sea Aquarium. The center, which rescues marine mammals and sea turtles, includes an aquarium, research laboratories, and educational programs.

Clermont: House of Presidents. Life-size wax

A shuttle launching at the Kennedy Space Center; it was from here that the U.S. launched its first satellite in 1958. The center draws more than 1.5 million visitors a year.

figures of the United States Presidents are displayed in period settings.

Coral Gables: Fairchild Tropical Garden. The gardens spread over 83 acres containing 5,000 varieties of tropical plants.

Dade City: Pioneer Florida Museum. Ten acres of old buildings contain thousands of artifacts, as well as an old train depot and engine.

Fort Lauderdale: Ocean World. Performing dolphins and sea lions are featured in the shows presented here.

Fort Myers: Edison Winter Home and Botanical Gardens. The House and guesthouse where Thomas A. Edison spent almost 50 winters are open to the public.

Gainesville: Marjorie Kinnan Rawlings State Historical Site. This farmhouse contains memorabilia of the author of *The Yearling.*

Hollywood: Six Flags—Atlantis. This 65-acre amusement park, with over

80 attractions, includes many water rides.

Homosassa Springs: Doll Museum. More than 1,700 antique and modern dolls are displayed here.

Kennedy Space Center: Spaceport USA. Here are films, displays, and tours of the facilities, including the Air Force Station and Museum, as well as the Missile Exhibit.

Key West: Ernest Hemingway Home and Museum. Built in 1851, this is the house where the author often wrote.

Kissimmee: Walt Disney World, Epcot Center, and MGM Studios. This world-famous complex is the chief attraction in Florida.

Lake Wales: The Bok Tower Gardens. The Bok Singing Tower, 205-feet high, provides bell music throughout the day.

Marineland: Marineland of Florida. Hundreds of fish of all sizes are on exhibit.

Miami Beach: Art Deco District. Some 800 buildings

The amazing performances of the dolphins and other aquatic creatures make Marineland a popular tourist attraction.

of early twentieth-century design can be seen in an area of one square mile.

Orlando: Sea World of Florida. The marine park features a huge aquarium and a killer whale show.

Palm Beach: Henry Morrison Flagler Museum. Built in 1901, the 55-room home of the railroad builder contains period furnishings and special collections.

Pensacola: Naval Air Station. The Naval Aviation Museum displays more than 100 full-size aircraft.

Perry: Cracker Homestead. Here is a homestead of double-notched squared logs and outbuildings from the early days of Florida.

St. Augustine: Spanish Quarter. The restoration of the colonial village of the 1700s includes several houses and a blacksmith shop.

Sarasota: Sarasota Jungle Gardens. The area contains more than 5,200 varieties of tropical plants and many tropical birds.

Tarpon Springs: Dodecanese Boulevard. Shrimp boats and sponge boats painted with Greek designs are anchored along this waterfront street.

Venice: Circus Winter Quarters. Here are a rehearsal hall and an arena in which are held occasional performances by the Ringling Bros. and Barnum and Bailey circus.

West Palm Beach: Lion Country Safari, Inc. One can drive a car through this 640-acre park, which contains more than 1,000 wild animals.

Winter Haven: Cypress Gardens. The great botanical gardens contain exotic plants and a theme park with varied areas.

Winter Park: The Charles Hosmer Morse Museum of American Art. There are fine examples of Tiffany glass in the large collection .

The Orange Bowl in Miami. The first Orange Bowl game, won by the University of Miami, was played in 1933.

Events

There are many events and organizations that schedule activities of various kinds in the state of Florida. Here are some of them.

Sports: Greyhound racing at Sanford-Orlando Kennel Club (Altamonte Springs); All-Florida Championship Rodeo (Arcadia); High Goal Polo (Boca Raton); greyhound racing at Naples-Fort Myers Greyhound Track (Bonita Springs); National Surfing Tourneys (Cocoa Beach); Junior Orange Bowl Festival (Coral Gables); auto races at Daytona International Speedway (Daytona Beach); greyhound racing at Daytona Beach Kennel Club (Daytona Beach); De Land-St. Johns River Festival (De Land); Deep-Sea Fishing Rodeo (Destin); Amateur Invitational Golf Tournament (Fernandina Beach); horse racing at Gulfstream Park (Fort Lauderdale); Southwest Florida Championship Rodeo (Fort Myers); horse racing at Hialeah Park (Hialeah); greyhound racing at Hollywood Greyhound Track (Hollywood): Rodeo and Frontier Days (Homestead); Sportfishing Festival (Islamorada); greyhound racing at Jacksonville Kennel Club (Jacksonville); Tournament Players Championship (Jacksonville Beach); Lipton International Players Championship (Key Biscayne); Silver Spurs Rodeo (Kissimmee); Key Colony Beach Sailfish Tournament (Marathon); Governor's Cup Rowing Regatta (Melbourne); Sun Dek Surfing Classic (Melbourne); Sebastian Offshore Sportfishing Tournament (Melbourne); greyhound racing at Flagler Dog Track (Miami); greyhound racing at Biscayne Dog Track (Miami); horse racing at Calder Race Course (Miami); Orange Bowl Game (Miami); Grand Prix of Miami (Miami); International Boat Show (Miami); Doral/Ryder Open PGA Golf Tournament (Miami); Miami/Budweiser Unlimited Hydroplace Regatta (Miami); Lee Evans Bowling Tournament (Miami); South Florida Auto Show (Miami); Speckled Perch Festival (Okeechobee); Cattleman's Rodeo (Okeechobee); Florida Citrus Sports Holiday (Orlando); harness racing at Ben White Raceway (Orlando); Antique Car

Meet (Ormond Beach); Palatka Horseman's Rodeo (Palatka); Captain Billfish Tournament (Panama City); Open Spearfishing Tournament (Panama City); Treasure Ship/Roy Martin King Mackerel Tournament (Panama City); greyhound racing at Ebro Greyhound Track (Panama City); Deep Sea Fishing Rodeo (Panama City Beach); Billfish Tournament (Pensacola); stock car racing at Five Flags Speedway (Pensacola); Pompano Beach Fishing Rodeo (Pompano Beach); harness racing at Pompano Park Raceway (Pompano Beach); auto racing at Sunshine Speedway (St. Petersburg); Southern Ocean Racing (St. Petersburg); greyhound racing at St. Petersburg Kennel Club (St. Petersburg); sailboat regattas (St. Petersburg); Sarasota Classic (Sarasota); Sarasota Sailing Squadron Labor Day Regatta (Sarasota); International Tarpon Tournament (Sarasota); Sebring 12-hour Endurance Race (Sebring); Hall of Fame Bowl (Tampa); greyhound racing at Tampa Track (Tampa); Walt Disney World Golf Classic (Lake Buena Vista); polo at Gulfstream Polo Field (West Palm Beach); greyhound racing at Palm Beach Kennel Club (West Palm Beach).

Arts and Crafts: Boynton's

GALA (Boynton Beach); Space Coast Art Festival (Cocoa Beach); Riverside Art Festival (Jacksonville); Coconut Grove Arts Festival (Miami); Art Deco Weekends (Miami Beach); Festival of the Arts (Miami Beach); Naples Shell Show (Naples); Images and Arts Fiesta (New Smyrna Beach); Azalea Festival (Palatka); Spring Festival of the Arts (Panama City); Great Gulfcoast Arts Festival (Pensacola); Sanibel Shell Fair (Sanibel Island).

Music: Florida Symphonic

Pops (Boca Raton); Florida Atlantic Theater (Boca Raton); the Florida Orchestra (Clearwater); Old Time Music Championship (Dade City); Philharmonic of Florida (Fort Lauderdale); Civic Music Concerts (Fort Lauderdale); Hollywood Festival of the Arts (Hollywood); Jazz Festival (Hollywood); Greater Hollywood Philharmonic Orchestra (Hollywood); Jacksonville Symphony (Jacksonville); Delius Festival (Jacksonville); Florida National

A violinist with the New World Symphony, this country's first and only full-time training orchestra.

Jazz Festival (Jacksonville); Bluegrass Festival (Kissimmee); Miami City Ballet (Miami); Greater Miami Opera Association (Miami); Orlando Opera Company (Orlando); Florida Symphony Orchestra (Orlando); Promenade Concerts (Palm Beach); Palm Beach Opera (Palm Beach); the Florida Orchestra (St. Petersburg); Florida Tournament of Bands (St. Petersburg); Sarasota Jazz Festival (Sarasota); Sarasota Opera Company (Sarasota); Music Festival of Florida (Sarasota); Concert Series (Sarasota); Summer Swamp Stomp (Tallahassee); Florida Orchestra (Tampa); Florida Folk Festival (White Springs); Jeanie Audition's and Ball (White Springs); Bach Festival (Winter Park).

Entertainment: Florida Seafood Festival (Apalachicola); De Soto County Fair and Livestock Exposition (Arcadia); Black Gold Jubilee Celebration (Belle Glade); Boca Festival Days (Boca Raton); Hernando County Fair (Brooksville); Seafood Festival (Cedar Key); Watermelon Festival (Chiefland); Fun 'n Sun Festival (Clearwater); Pasco County Fair (Dade City); Pioneer Florida Festival (Dade City); Cracker Day (Deerfield Beach); Chautauqua Festival Day (De Runiak Springs); Manatee

Festival (De Land); Central Florida Balloon Classic (De Land); Volusia County Fair and Youth Show (De Land); Turn-of-the-Century Holiday (De Land); Bon Festival (Delray Beach); Seafood Festival (Destin); Highland Games and Scottish Festival (Dunedin); Isle of Eight Flags Shrimp Festival (Fernandina Beach); Southwest Florida Fair (Fort Myers); Pageant of Light (Fort Myers); Shrimp Festival (Fort Myers Beach); St. Lucie County Fair (Fort Pierce); Seafood Festival

(Fort Walton Beach); Billy Bowlegs Festival (Fort Walton Beach); Animal Day (Gainesville); Heritage Fair (Gainesville); Museum Open House (Gainesville); Florida Derby Festival (Hallandale); Seminole Indian Tribal Fair (Hallandale); Hollywood Sun 'n Fun Festival (Hollywood); Broward County Fair (Hollywood); Indian Key Festival (Islamorada); Gator Bowl Festival (Jacksonville); Beaches Festival Weekend Celebration (Jacksonville Beach);

Located in one of Miami's oldest neighborhoods, the Coconut Grove Playhouse was built in 1926 and held its first theatrical season in 1956. Most of its productions are premiers.

Leif Erikson Day Pageant (Jensen Beach); Turtle Watch (Jensen Beach); Official Florida State Air Fair (Kissimmee); Boating Jamboree (Kissimmee); Battle of Olustee Reenactment (Lake City); North Florida Air Show (Lake City); Columbia County Fair (Lake City); Sun and Fun EAA Fly-in (Lakeland); Grant Seafood Festival (Melbourne); Turtle Crawl (Melbourne); Orange Bowl Festival (Miami); Carnival Miami/ Calle Ocho Festival (Miami); Italian Renaissance Festival (Miami); International Festival (Miami); Miccosukee Indian Arts Festival (Miami); Collier County Agricultural Fair (Naples); Chasco Fiesta (New Port Richey); Southeastern Youth Fair (Ocala); Orlando Scottish Highland Games (Orlando); Central Florida Fair (Orlando); Pioneer Days Folk Festival (Orlando); Putnam County Fair (Palatka); Flagler Anniversary Open House (Palm Beach); Bay County Fair (Panama City); Indian Summer Seafood Festival (Panama City Beach); Mardi Gras (Pensacola); Fiesta of the Five Flags (Pensacola); Creek Indian Pow-Wow (Pensacola); Blue Angel Air Show (Pensacola); Florida Forest Festival (Perry);

Seafood Festival (Pompano Beach); Boat Parade (Pompano Beach); Blessing of the Fishing Fleet (St. Augustine); Spanish Night Watch (St. Augustine); Greek Landing Day Festival (St. Augustine); Days in Spain (St. Augustine); Maritime Festival (St. Augustine); British Night Watch (St. Augustine); Holiday Regatta of Lights (St. Augustine); International Folk Fair (St. Petersburg); Renaissance Festival (St. Petersburg); Festival of States (St. Petersburg); Medieval Fair (Sarasota); Bradford County Fair (Starke); Martin County Fair (Stuart); Battle Reenactment (Tallahassee); Flying High Circus (Tallahassee); Springtime Tallahassee (Tallahassee); Spring Farm Days (Tallahassee); North Florida Fair (Tallahassee); December on the Farm (Tallahassee); Florida State Fair (Tampa); Gasparilla Pirate Invasion (Tampa); Festival of Epiphany (Tarpon Springs); Valiant Air Command Air Show (Titusville); Venetian Sun Fiesta (Venice); South Florida Fair and Exposition (West Palm Beach); Sunfest (West Palm Beach); Florida Citrus Festival and Polk County Fair (Winter Haven).

Tours: Historic Home Tour (Jacksonville); Old Island Days (Key West); Garden Club Tour of Homes (St. Augustine).

Theater: Caldwell Playhouse (Boca Raton); Florida Shakespeare Festival (Coral Gables); Parker Playhouse (Fort Lauderdale); Passion Play (Lake Wales); Coconut Grove Playhouse (Miami); Jackie Gleason Theater of the Performing Arts (Miami Beach); Royal Poinciana Playhouse (Palm Beach); "Cross and Sword" (St. Augustine); The Players of Sarasota (Sarasota); Asolo Performing Arts Center (Sarasota).

Participants in the Turtle Watch on Jensen Beach have the rare opportunity to observe the giant turtles nesting in the sand.

Florida is a peninsula, with more than 1,350 miles of coastline. Many of the beaches in the northwest, from Panama City to Pensacola, are covered with dazzling white sands that stretch for miles along the Gulf of Mexico.

The Land and the Climate

Florida is the nation's tropical area, surrounded by warm coastal waters. The peninsular state has three major land regions: the Atlantic Coastal Plain, the East Gulf Coastal Plain, and the Florida Uplands.

The Atlantic Coastal Plain is part of that vast strip of shoreline that extends northward to New Jersey. This plain covers the entire eastern part of the state, ranging in width from 30 to 100 miles. This is a low, level plain with a narrow ribbon of sand bars, coral reefs, and islands in the Atlantic Ocean, just beyond the mainland. Between this ribbon and the mainland are long shallow lakes, lagoons, rivers, and bays. On the mainland are marshes that stretch for miles inland.

At left:
Swamps, marshes, and bogs are some of the most common features of southern Florida. The subtropical Everglades in the south cover more than 5,000 square miles of the state with swampy grasslands.

Below:
The sun sets on the eastern coast. Lagoons that often narrow into marshy inlets fringe much of the Atlantic shore.

Above:
Because much of Florida's topography and climate are unique in the United States, rare and exotic forms of wildlife are found in the state. Alligators and flamingos, among many other species, live in the high grass and marshes of the Everglades, making it one of America's greatest wildlife preserves.

At right:
Miami's cageless Metrozoo allows wild animals to roam free. They are separated from visitors by a system of moats.

Much of southern Florida is covered by the Big Cypress Swamp and the Everglades—the latter covering some 5,000 square miles of the state with its swampy grasslands. The Florida Keys, off the southern tip of the state, are a series of islands curving to the southwest for about 200 miles.

Many kinds of agriculture are supported by the Atlantic Coastal Plain. Fruits, vegetables, beef cattle, dairy cattle, and forest products are grown here. There is some stone quarrying at the southern tip of the mainland.

The East Gulf Coastal Plain begins at the Gulf of Mexico on the west coast of Florida, extending west to Mississippi and north to southern Illinois. In Florida, the plain has two main sections. One portion covers the southwestern part of the peninsula, joining the Atlantic Coastal Plain at the center of the state, in the middle of the Everglades and the Big Cypress Swamp. The other section curves around the northern edge of the Gulf of Mexico, extending along the Panhandle to the western border of the state. As with the Atlantic Coastal Plain, long, narrow islands occur along the Gulf Coast, with large coastal swamps extending inland. Agriculture here is similar to that of the Atlantic Coastal Plain, while the Gulf of Mexico provides both fish and sponges to the Florida economy.

A view of Jacksonville at night. Located in the northeast, it is Florida's largest city and a major business center.

Miami, on the southeast coast, with its mild temperatures and inviting beaches, has long been one of America's most popular vacation spots.

A picturesque sunset in Tampa, the state's third largest city. It is located on the central west coast, a region that contains one of the state's richest deposits of phosphate rock and other heavy minerals.

On the map, the Florida Uplands look something like a giant arm and hand. A finger of the hand points down the center of the state toward the southern tip of the peninsula. The rest of it runs across the Panhandle above the East Gulf Coastal Plain to the western border. The Uplands separate the two sections of the East Gulf Coastal Plain from each other and from the Atlantic Coastal Plain. Many of the state's citrus crops—oranges, grapefruit, and tangerines—are grown in this region.

The coastline of Florida is 1,350 miles long, with the Atlantic Coast measuring 580 miles and the Gulf Coast 770 miles. But when all the shoreline of the sounds, bays, and offshore islands are added in, the coastline on the Atlantic side is 3,331 miles long and the Gulf Coast measures 5,095 miles. Biscayne Bay, just south of Miami, is the most important bay on the Atlantic side. On the Gulf side, the major bays are Charlotte Harbor, Sarasota Bay, and Tampa Bay. Along the Panhandle are Apalachee, St. Joseph, St. Andrew, Choctawhatchee, and Pensacola Bays.

The largest river in the state is the St. Johns River, which begins near Lake Okeechobee and flows 275 miles northward, roughly parallel to the Atlantic Coast. Other important rivers are the St. Marys, the Perdido, the Apalachicola, and the Suwannee. The largest lake in Florida is Lake Okeechobee. It covers about 700 square miles and is the second largest natural lake in the country that is wholly within the United States. Only Lake Michigan is larger. Throughout central Florida there are about 30,000 shallow lakes—most of them only a few acres in area.

Florida's climate ranges from humid subtropical at the southern tip to temperate in the northern areas. Even in midsummer, the heat is moderated by cooling Atlantic and Gulf breezes. Temperatures in summer average about the same throughout the state—83 degrees Fahrenheit—but in winter, Miami averages 67 degrees F. while temperatures drop to 56 degrees F. in northern Florida. Rainfall averages 53 inches per year, some of it coming with the hurricanes whose paths cut across Florida.

The History

Evidence from burial mounds found along the western coast of Florida indicates that prehistoric Indians may have lived in the area as long as 10,000 years ago. When white men first came to the region, there were about 10,000 Indians in what was to become the state of Florida. These natives belonged to four major tribes. The Calusa and the Tegesta in the south were hunters and fishermen, while the Timucuan in the central and northeast section, and the Apalachee in the northeast, were farmers and hunters.

In 1513 the Spanish explorer Juan Ponce de León, in search of the legendary Fountain of Youth, landed on the eastern coast and claimed the region for Spain. He named the land Florida, for the colorful tropical flowers that grew there abundantly (*flor* is the Spanish word for flower). Returning to Florida in 1521 to found a colony, de León was

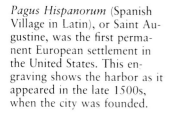

Pagus Hispanorum (Spanish Village in Latin), or Saint Augustine, was the first permanent European settlement in the United States. This engraving shows the harbor as it appeared in the late 1500s, when the city was founded.

Spanish explorer Juan Ponce de León set sail from Puerto Rico in March 1513 in search of the legendary Fountain of Youth. He landed near present-day St. Augustine on April 2, and christened the land La Florida, probably because he had discovered it during the season of *Pascua Florida,* or "Flowery Easter." He then sailed down the east coast and around the tip of the peninsula, exploring the lower west coast before returning to Puerto Rico in September. A year later, in Spain, the explorer was granted permission to colonize Florida, but he was unable to return until 1521. At that time, with two ships, farm animals, agricultural tools, and about 200 men, he landed on the west coast, probably at what is now Charlotte Harbor. There Ponce de León was wounded in an Indian attack, and his expedition sailed to Cuba, where he died of his wounds.

severely wounded by Indians in a battle. He and his men left the region, but the explorer died soon afterward.

Pánfilo de Narváez, another Spanish explorer, arrived with some 400 men on Florida's southwestern coast in 1528 and traveled north looking for gold. Shipwrecks killed him and most of his men. Still another Spanish explorer, Hernando de Soto, arrived near the Tampa Bay area in 1539. He led his men across west central Florida and discovered the Mississippi River.

It wasn't until 20 years after de Soto's arrival that any attempts were made to colonize Florida. A trial settlement in Pensacola failed, but in 1564 a group of French Protestants, called Huguenots, founded a colony on the St. Johns River and built Fort Caroline near what is now Jacksonville. When King Philip II of Spain learned of this French incursion into what he considered Spanish territory, he sent a sea captain, Don Pedro Menéndez de Avilés, to drive out the French. The Spanish expedition arrived in 1565 and founded St. Augustine, the first permanent European settlement in what is now the United States. The Spaniards also massacred the Huguenots, thus ending French attempts to settle in eastern Florida.

Fort Matanzas, on Rattle-snake Island, off the northeast coast near St. Augustine, was the site of a bloody clash between French and Spanish colonists in 1565. By the time the battle was over, more than 300 Huguenots (French Protestants) had been killed. *Matanzas* is the Spanish word for "slaughter."

For almost 200 years, the Spanish tried to impose a European way of life on the Florida Indians. Meanwhile, the English were setting up colonies north of the territory, and the French were settling to the west. When war broke out between the British and the French in the mid-1700s, Spain took the side of the French. Then, in 1763, the English captured the Caribbean Island of Cuba, and Spain traded Florida to them for Cuba.

The English promptly divided their new territory into two separate colonies, East and West Florida. Most of the region was included in West Florida, which stretched from the area west of the Apalachicola River through parts of what are now Alabama, Mississippi, and Louisiana. East Florida included the rest of the peninsula.

During the American Revolution, Spanish troops took advantage of the conflict and marched into West Florida in 1779. The English, weakened by the war, surrendered West Florida to Spain in 1781; two years later the Spanish regained all their former territory. The second Spanish period lasted until 1821.

In the early 1800s, Florida was the only part of southeastern North America that did not belong to the United States. As a result, runaway slaves, escaped criminals, and Indians who rebelled against white efforts to displace them sought refuge there. The settlers in Florida wanted to join the Republic, but the Spanish refused to sell to the United States. In 1812 some eastern Florida settlers revolted and declared their independence, but the Spaniards put down the uprising. During the War of 1812, Spain let the British use Pensacola as a naval base, and in 1814 General Andrew Jackson led his troops into Florida, capturing Pensacola.

Jackson and his men were back in Florida during the First Seminole War (1816–18), capturing Fort St. Marks on the Gulf of Mexico during this war against the Florida Indians. Jackson then marched east to the Suwannee River, defeating the Seminoles there. In 1819 Spain turned Florida over to the United States after the Federal Government agreed to pay $5 million to American citizens for property damage.

General Andrew Jackson became a hero in the War of 1812 partly as a result of his capture of Pensacola in 1814. In the First Seminole War, Jackson routed the Seminole Indians and destroyed their villages, in the belief that these villages were havens for runaway slaves and outlaws. Jackson's aggressive tactics in this region may well have frightened Spain into ceding Florida to the United States in 1819.

Florida finally became a United States territory in 1822, and thousands of settlers poured in, but they found that there was little land on which to settle, since the native Seminole Indians owned some of the richest farmland. The Federal Government offered the Seminoles land in the Oklahoma region (designated Indian Territory), and some of the Indians agreed to go West, but most refused to leave their land. A band of Seminoles massacred Major Francis L. Dade and his U.S. Army troops near Bushnell in 1835, triggering the Second Seminole War, which lasted until 1842. Inevitably, the Seminoles were defeated, and most of them left Florida, but a small band stayed behind (Not until 1934 did these remaining Seminoles sign a peace treaty with the U.S. Government.)

Florida was finally admitted to the Union as a slave state in 1845. At the time, it had a population of about 66,500 people, most of whom owned small farms. On January 10, 1861, Florida withdrew, or seceded, from the Union after the election of Abraham Lincoln as president. On February 8, Florida joined the Confederate States of America.

A lithograph by L. Grozelieu of Key West, circa 1855. On an island at the southwestern extremity of the Florida Keys, Key West is the southernmost city in the continental United States.

A depiction of the Civil War battle at Natural Bridge. Here, in 1865, Confederate troops inflicted heavy casualties on the Union Army in a successful defense of Tallahassee, the only uncaptured Southern capital east of the Mississippi.

During the Civil War (1861–65), most of Florida's coastal towns were captured by Union forces, but Confederate troops won the Battle of Olustee—one of the few major battles fought on Florida soil—on February 20, 1864. In March 1865 a small band of young boys and old men, with a handful of Confederate soldiers, successfully defended Tallahassee against Union troops. As a result, Tallahassee and Austin, Texas, were the only Confederate state capitals that Federal troops did not capture.

After the Civil War, Florida was occupied by Union forces during the Reconstruction period. It was not readmitted to the Union until 1868. In the 1880s, the state's economy began to boom. Large phosphate deposits were discovered. The swamplands were being drained for farming. New land opened for development. Citrus-fruit groves were planted, and resorts sprang up along both coasts, offering their warm climate and beautiful beaches.

In the early part of the twentieth century, hundreds of thousands of land speculators flooded into the state of Florida. The population grew at an enormous rate, and seven new counties were formed in 1921. In 1926 the bubble burst when a depression hit. Banks closed, people lost their money, and two severe hurricanes in 1926 and 1928 killed hundreds. No sooner had Florida recovered from this disaster than the world was plunged into the Great Depression of the 1930s, which brought more bank failures, unemployment, and foreclosures on farmland.

Then came World War II (1941–45). Because so much of Florida bordered the Atlantic Ocean it was seen as subject to enemy attack, yet vital to the defense of the country. Several air and naval bases were set up in the state, in addition to the long-established base at Pensacola.

After the war, industrial expansion came to Florida. Manufacturing income rose almost as high as income from tourism, as the state's mineral resources—phosphate, crushed stone, cement, sand, and gravel—were developed more fully. Jacksonville and Port Everglades became busy centers of commerce. In the 1950s, Cape Canaveral (later Cape Kennedy) became a major space and rocket center, as well as one of Florida's leading tourist attractions. The population almost doubled between 1950 and 1960, and increased at the same rate during the next 20 years.

Some of the oldest remnants of American culture in the continental United States are preserved in Florida cities like St. Augustine. Some parts of the state, especially the Everglades, are as untamed as they were when the Spanish explorers arrived. Today Florida attracts many new residents and visitors every year with fishing facilities, hotels and resorts. Its relaxed atmosphere goes hand in hand with a progressive economy that offers many employment opportunities, from agriculture to electronics.

Education

The British organized the first schools in Florida in the 1770s in Pensacola and St. Augustine. The Constitution of 1868 established a public school system for white and black children. In the 1950s Florida achieved desegregation of the public schools in a more timely manner than most of the southern states. All public schools are now desegregated, though many students are bused throughout the state. In 1853 the first institution of higher learning in Florida was the East Florida Seminary, now known as the University of Florida.

The People

Over 90 percent of Floridians live in metropolitan areas. Many people retire to Florida because of its warm climate and recreational activities. This has given the state a relatively high percentage of older residents. Most Floridians were born in the United States. Those who were born in foreign countries came primarily from Cuba, Canada, England, Germany, and Russia. Since the 1950s, Cuban immigrants have comprised one of Florida's newest and most powerful ethnic groups. During the last three decades Cuban culture has become firmly anchored in many parts of the state, and has had a significant influence on the foods, language, and politics of Florida. Baptists make up the largest religious group in the state. Other prominent denominations are the Roman Catholic, Methodist, Episcopal, and Presbyterian.

At left:
Although most of the Seminole Indians were moved to Oklahoma in 1842, a handful still populate parts of southeastern Florida. The tribe was formed in the middle of the 18th century by Creek refugees, members of other southeastern tribes, and escaped slaves. The Seminole lived primarily by raising corn, sugar cane, sweet potatoes, and beans in addition to hunting and fishing.

Below:
Miami is one of Florida's fastest-growing metropolitan areas. During the past few decades, the region has seen a substantial increase in Cuban immigration, making Hispanic culture an influential part of daily life.

Famous People

Many famous people were born in the state of Florida. Here are a few:

Julian "Cannonball" Adderley 1928-1975, Tampa. Jazz saxophonist

Elizabeth Ashley b.1941, Ocala. Stage and film actress: *Ship of Fools, Coma*

Pat Boone b.1934, Jacksonville. Pop singer

Don Carter b.1930, Miami. Championship bowler

Jacqueline Cochran 1910-1980, Pensacola. First woman flyer to exceed the speed of sound

Faye Dunaway b.1941, Bascom. Academy Award-winning actress: *Network*

Chris Evert b.1954, Fort Lauderdale. Champion tennis player

Steve Garvey b.1948, Tampa. Baseball player

Artis Gilmore b.1949, Chipley. Basketball player

Bobby Goldsboro b.1942, Marianna. Country-and-western singer

Dwight Gooden b. 1964, Tampa. Baseball pitcher

Deacon Jones b.1938, Eatonville. Football player

Edmund Kirby-Smith 1824-1893, St. Augustine. Last Confederate commander to surrender

Butterfly McQueen b.1911, Tampa. Film actress: *Gone With The Wind, The Mosquito Coast*

At her death, Jacqueline Cochran held more speed, altitude, and distance records than any other pilot, male or female.

After the fall of the Confederacy, Edmund Kirby-Smith became president of the University of Nashville and later taught mathematics at the University of the South.

Charles E. Merrill 1885-1956, Green Cove Springs. Broker and co-founder of Merrill Lynch brokerage

Patrick O'Neal b.1927, Ocala. Film and television actor: *The Way We Were, The Stepford Wives*

Charles H. Percy b. 1919, Pensacola. U.S. Senator

Sidney Poitier b.1927, Miami.

Academy Award-winning actor: *Lilies of the Field, Guess Who's Coming to Dinner*

A. Philip Randolph 1889-1979, Crescent City. Civil rights leader

Esther Rolle b.1933, Pompano Beach. Television actress: *Maude, Good Times*

Charles E. Merrill was also one of the founders of Family Circle *magazine, which began publication in 1932.*

Joseph "Vinegar Joe" Stilwell 1883-1946, Palatka. World War II general

Ben Vereen b.1946, Miami. Dancer and actor: *Roots, Tenspeed and Brown Shoe*

Jack Youngblood b.1950, Monticello. Football player

Colleges and Universities

There are many colleges and universities in Florida. Here are the more prominent, with their locations, dates of founding, and enrollments.

Barry University, Miami Shores, 1940, 6,466.

Bethune-Cookman College, Daytona Beach, 1872, 2,301.

Flagler College, St. Augustine, 1963, 1,275.

Florida Agricultural and Mechanical University, Tallahassee, 1887, 9,508.

Florida Atlantic University, Boca Raton, 1964, 14,778.

Florida Institute of Technology, Melbourne, 1958, 5,826.

Florida International University, Miami, 1965, 19,142.

A. Philip Randolph published the Messenger, *a radical black magazine, and was instrumental in ending segregation in defense plants and the military.*

Florida Southern College, Lakeland, 1885, 2,604.

Florida State University, Tallahassee, 1857, 28,512.

Jacksonville University, Jacksonville, 1934, 2,567.

Lynn University, Boca Raton, 1962, 1,200.

Rollins College, Winter Park, 1885, 2,093.

St. Thomas University, Miami, 1961, 2,703.

Stetson University, De Land, 1883, 3,069.

University of Florida, Gainesville, 1853, 34,361.

University of Miami, Coral Gables, 1925, 13,857.

University of North Florida, Jacksonville, 1965, 9,073.

University of South Florida, Tampa, 1956, 34,161.

University of Tampa, Tampa, 1931, 2,506.

University of West Florida, Pensacola, 1967, 7,941.

Where to Get More Information

Florida Division of Tourism Visitor Inquiry
126 Van Buren Street
Tallahassee, Florida 32399-2000
or call, 1-904-487-1462

Mississippi

The great seal of the state of Mississippi was adopted in 1817. It is circular and bears the figure of an eagle holding an olive branch (representing peace) in its right talon and three arrows (representing war) in its left. Around the circle is inscribed "The Great Seal of the State of Mississippi."

MISSISSIPPI

TENNESSEE

Corinth

Holly Springs • HOLLY
SPRINGS
NATIONAL
FOREST New Albany

Clarksdale • Oxford Tupelo

ARKANSAS

HOLLY SPRINGS
NATIONAL FOREST TOMBIGBEE
NATIONAL
FOREST • Amory
• Aberdeen

Cleveland

Grenada

SCOTT ■

Indianola West Point •

Greenwood Starkville •

Greenville • Leland TOMBIGBEE
NATIONAL FOREST **Columbus**

Kosciusko • Louisville

DELTA
NATIONAL
FOREST • Yazoo City

• Philadelphia

Canton •

LOUISIANA **Vicksburg** BIENVILLE
NATIONAL
FOREST **Meridian**

Pearl •

Jackson ★

ALABAMA

Natchez • Brookhaven **Laurel** • DE SOTO
NATIONAL
FOREST

HOMOCHITTO
NATIONAL
FOREST **Hattiesburg** •

N
△

McComb • • Columbia

DE SOTO
NATIONAL
FOREST

LOUISIANA

Picayune • Ocean
Springs • • Moss Point

Bay Saint Louis • **Biloxi** ■ Pascagoula

Gulfport SHIP
ISLAND *GULF OF
MEXICO*

Mississippi River

★ State Capital
● Cities or towns
■ OF SPECIAL INTEREST

0 10 20 40 60 80 100 120 140 160 180 Miles
0 10 20 40 60 80 100 120 140 160 180 200 250 300 Kilometres

Capital: Jackson

State Flower: Magr

MISSISSIPPI
At a Glance

State Flag

Major Industries: Manufacturing, food processing, agriculture, forest products, fishing

Major Crops: Soybeans, cotton, rice, timber

State Bird: Mockingbird

State Tree: Magnolia

Nickname: Magnolia State

State Song: "Go, Mississippi!"

State Motto: *Virtute et Armis* (By valor and arms)

Size: 47,689 square miles (32nd largest)
Population: 2,614,294 (31st largest)

State Flag

The state flag of Mississippi, adopted in 1894, shows the state's ties both to the United States and the Confederacy. In the upper left corner, with a red background, are two diagonal lines of blue with 13 stars on them—a representation of the Confederate battle flag. The rest of the flag carries wide stripes of red, white, and blue—the colors of the flag of the United States.

State Motto

Virtute et Armis

The Latin motto means "by valor and arms" and was suggested in 1894.

Dunlieth is a National Historic Landmark and is one of more than 500 antebellum homes in Natchez.

State Name and Nicknames

The state of Mississippi was named after the Mississippi River, which had several other names. Gulf Coast Indians called the river the Malbouchia, while the Spanish discoverers called it Rio del Espíritu Santo and Rio Grande de Florida. Later, the French named it the Colbert and the St. Louis River. Indians in the northwest called it the Mississippi, a Chippewa Indian word meaning "Large River"; that name appears on LaSalle's map of 1695.

The most common nickname for Mississippi is the *Magnolia State* because there are so many of those trees in the state. But it is also known as the *Eagle State* and the *Border-Eagle State* since there is an eagle on the state seal. There are so many bayous in the state that it has been named the *Bayou State*. And because of the multitude of catfish in its streams and swamps Mississippi is called the *Mud-Cat State*.

State Capital

The first capital of Mississippi was Natchez (1798-1802), followed by Washington (1802-1817), Natchez again (1817-1821), and Columbia (1821-1822). Finally, in 1822, Jackson was selected as the permanent capital.

State Flower

In 1900, the children of Mississippi voted the flower of the magnolia tree, *Magnolia grandiflora*, the state flower. However, the state legislature did not adopt it officially until 1952.

State Tree

Magnolia grandiflora, the magnolia, was named the state tree in 1938. It is also called the evergreen magnolia.

State Bird

The mockingbird, *Mimus polyglottos*, was selected as the state bird of Mississippi in 1944.

State Waterfowl

Aix sponsa, the wood duck, was named the state waterfowl in 1974.

State Beverage

Milk was selected as the state beverage in 1984.

State Fish

In 1974, the largemouth bass, *Micropterus salmoides*, was adopted as the state fish.

State Fossil

The prehistoric whale was named the state fossil in 1981.

State Insect

Adopted in 1980, the honey bee, *Apis mellifera*, is the state insect.

State Land Mammal

The white-tailed deer, *Odocoileus virginianus*, was selected as the Mississippi land mammal in 1974.

State Shell

In 1974, the oyster shell was named the state shell.

State Water Mammal

The bottlenosed dolphin, *Tursiops truncatus*, was selected as state water mammal in 1974.

State Song

The state song, selected in 1962, is "Go, Mississippi," written by Houston Davis.

Population

The population of Mississippi in 1992 was 2,614,294, making it the 31st most populous state. There are 58.7 persons per square mile—30 percent of the population live in metropolitan areas. Over 99 percent of Mississippians were born in the United States.

Industries

The principal industries of the state of Mississippi are food processing, seafood, trade, and agriculture. The chief manufactured products are apparel, lumber and wood products, food products, electrical machinery and equipment, and transportation equipment.

Agriculture

The chief crops of the state are cotton, soybeans, and rice. Mississippi is also a livestock state. There are estimated to be 1.3 million cattle, 149,000 hogs and pigs, and 456.5 million broilers on its farms. Pine, oak, and hardwoods are harvested.

Sand, gravel, clay, and crushed stone are important mineral resources. Commercial fishing earned $31.3 million in 1992.

Government

The governor of Mississippi is elected to a four-year term, as are the lieutenant governor, the secretary of state, the treasurer, the state auditor of public accounts,

The "Mighty Mississippi" still provides a passage for riverboat cruises, much as it did a hundred years ago.

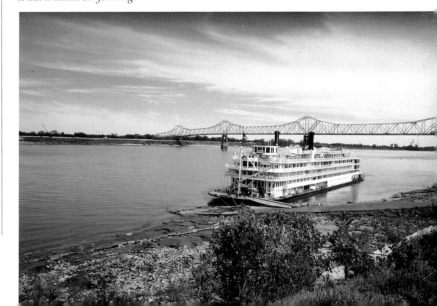

the superintendent of education, the attorney general, and the commissioners of agriculture and commerce, insurance, and land. The state legislature, which meets annually, consists of a 52-member senate and a 122-member house of representatives. They are elected to four-year terms. The most recent state constitution was adopted in 1890. In addition to its two U.S. senators, Mississippi has five representatives in the U.S. House of Representatives. The state has seven votes in the electoral college.

Sports

Many sporting events on the collegiate and secondary school levels are scheduled all over the state. The University of Mississippi and Mississippi State University are perennial national foot-ball powers, and both schools have appeared in numerous post-season bowl games.

All of this country's space shuttles are tested at the John C. Stennis Space Center in Hancock County.

Major Cities

Biloxi (population 46,319). Settled in 1699, this is the oldest town in the Mississippi Valley. It has been a popular resort since the 1840s; even today, although it is a leading oyster and shrimp fishing center, it is an exquisite city, with magnolia trees, camellias, azaleas, roses, and crepe myrtle blooming along the streets, and oaks draped with Spanish moss.

Things to see in Biloxi: Beauvoir-Jefferson Davis Shrine, the Biloxi Lighthouse (1848), the Old Biloxi Cemetery, the Tullis-Toledano Manor (1856), Deer Island, Keesler Air Force Base, Small Craft Harbor, and the Vieux Marche Walking Tour.

Jackson (population 196,637). Founded in 1821, the capital city was built in the center of the state. It was laid out in a checkerboard pattern at the suggestion of Thomas Jefferson, and the original plans called for the reservation of every other square as a park or green. In 1863 the city was reduced to ashes by Union General William T. Sherman, bringing it the nickname "Chimneyville." But it was rebuilt, and today it is a city of charm.

Things to see in Jackson: the State Capitol (1903), the Governor's Mansion (1842), the State Historical Museum, the Confederate Monument (1891), the Archives and History Building, the Oaks (1846), the Manship House

(1857), the Museum of Natural Science, the Municipal Art Gallery, the Mississippi Museum of Art, the Mynelle Gardens, the Jackson Zoological Park, Battlefield Park, the Mississippi Agriculture and Forestry Museum and National Agricultural Aviation Museum, and the Mississippi Petrified Forest.

Meridian (population 41,036). Settled in 1831, Meridian is an industrial, agricultural, and retailing center.

Thing to see in Meridian: Merrehope (1858), the Frank W. Williams House (1886), the Meridian Museum of Art, the Jimmie Rodgers Museum, and the Naval Air Station.

Places to Visit

Clarksdale: Delta Blues Museum. Memorabilia, videotapes, and slide programs of blues music are displayed.

Columbus: Historic homes. There are more than 100 homes in Columbus that date to before the Civil War, and several are open to visitors.

Corinth: Curlee House.

Built in 1857, it served as headquarters for generals Bragg, Halleck, and Hood during the Civil War.

Greenville: River Road Queen. This is a replica of a nineteenth-century paddlewheel steamboat.

Greenwood: Florewood River Plantation. Crops are worked and harvested at this recreation of a plantation of the 1850s.

Grenada: Historic Old Grenada. This is a motor and walking tour of old homes

and churches.

Gulfport: National Space Technology Laboratories. This is the second-largest NASA field station in the United States.

Natchez: Historic Springfield Plantation. Believed to be the oldest mansion in Mississippi, the house, with its hand-carved woodwork, was built between 1786 and 1790.

Ocean Springs: Shearwater Pottery. A fine pottery, established in 1928, displays

An aerial view of Jackson, Mississippi.

Rowan Oak, William Faulkner's home, features a wall on which he wrote the outline to his Pulitzer Prize-winning novel The Fable.

glazedware created by the founder.

Oxford: Rowan Oak. Once the home of the novelist William Faulkner, the house contains original furnishings and memorabilia.

Pascagoula: Old Spanish Fort and Museum. Built by the French in 1718, it is the oldest fortified structure in the Mississippi Valley.

Port Gibson: First Presbyterian Church. Built in 1859, it contains chandeliers from the steamboat *Robert E. Lee.*

Tupelo: Elvis Presley Park and Birthplace. In a park stands the small frame house where the singer lived the first three years of his life.

Vicksburg: McRaven Home Civil War Tour. Heavily shelled during the Siege of Vicksburg in 1863, this home is an architectural record of Vicksburg history.

Woodville: Rosemont Plantation. Built around 1810, this was the home of Jefferson Davis and his family.

Yazoo City: Wister Gardens. Fourteen acres of azaleas, roses, tulips, crysanthemums, hyacinths, jonquils, crocuses, camellias, sasanquas, hollies, and other flowers are open to the public.

Events

There are many events and organizations that schedule activities of various kinds in the state of Mississippi. Here are some of them.

Sports: Mississippi Deep-Sea Fishing Rodeo (Gulfport); Mississippi State Horse Show (Jackson).

Arts and Crafts: Delta Jubilee (Clarksdale).

Music: Delta Blues Festival (Greenville); Jackson Symphony (Jackson); Lively Arts Festival (Meridian); Jimmie Rodgers Memorial Festival (Meridian).

Entertainment: Mardi Gras (Biloxi); Shrimp Festival (Biloxi); Seafood Festival (Biloxi); Deep South Festival (Columbus); Civil War Living History Expo (Holy Springs); Dixie National Livestock Show (Jackson); Mississippi State Fair (Jackson); Central Mississippi Fair and State Dairy Show (Kosciusko); Lighted Azalea Trail (Louisville); Southeast Mississippi State Fair (Meridian); Faulkner Conference (Oxford); Mardi Gras (Pascagoula); Landing of D'Iberville (Pascagoula); Flagship Festival (Pascagoula); Jackson County Air Show (Pascagoula); Jackson County Fair (Pascagoula); Mardi Gras (Pass Christian); Blessing of the Fleet (Pass Christian); Choctaw Indian Fair (Philadelphia); Neshoba County Fair (Philadelphia); Tobacco Spit in Billy John Crumpton's Pasture (Raleigh).

Tours: Garden Club Pilgrimage (Biloxi); Pilgrimage (Columbus); Spring Pilgrimage (Gulfport); Pilgrimage (Holly Springs); Pilgrimage (Natchez); Spring Pilgrimage (Vicksburg).

Each year, thousands of tourists visit this two-room house in Tupelo where Elvis Presley was born.

The Mississippi River, seen here at Vicksburg, is the major river of the United States. It served as an artery of transportation for the Indians, then for explorers, trappers, traders, and settlers. With the advent of steamboats in the early 1800s, it became one of the most important trade and transportation routes in the country. The Mississippi had great strategic value during the Civil War, and the Union victory at Vicksburg was a turning point in the conflict.

The Land and the Climate

Because of the influence of both the Gulf of Mexico and the Mississippi River, the nation's major waterway, the state of Mississippi is a study in contrasts. It has two main land regions: the Mississippi Alluvial Plain and the East Gulf Coastal Plain.

The Mississippi Alluvial Plain covers the entire western edge of the state (alluvia are sediments deposited by flowing water). The region is narrow south of Vicksburg, but widens to the north, covering the area from the Mississippi River east to the Yazoo, Tallahatchie, and Coldwater Rivers. In these fertile lowlands, called the Delta, cotton, grains, soybeans, and cattle are raised.

Cotton is harvested in the fertile region known as the Delta, which contains soil enriched by silt that was deposited during Mississippi River floods. Grains, soybeans, and cattle are other farm products of this area, which is also called the Mississippi Alluvial Plain.

A lighthouse stands in Biloxi Harbor, "Shrimp Capital" of the nation. Biloxi Bay, on the southern shore, is the largest bay in Mississippi.

The East Gulf Coastal Plain comprises the territory east of the Delta; it is made up of low, forested hills. Toward the west the land is covered with loess, or yellowish–brown soil blown by the winds, and natives call this area the Cane, Bluff, or Loess Hills. Northeastern Mississippi contains the Tennessee River Hills, where the highest point in the comparatively flat state is located, 806-foot Woodall Mountain. The Pine Hills, or Piney Woods, are in the southeastern part of this region. The main prairie of the area, called the Black Belt or Black Prairie for its rich, dark soil, stretches through 10 counties in the northeast. Its chief products are livestock, corn, and hay.

Mississippi has a salt-water coastline along the Gulf of Mexico that extends for 44 miles measured in a straight line. If the coastline of the bays and coves are added, the seashore is 359 miles long. The largest bays are Biloxi, St. Louis, and Pascagoula, all of which have port cities with resort facilities.

The Mississippi River forms most of the western border of the state. Other important rivers are the Big Black, Yazoo, Coldwater, Sunflower, Tallahatchie, Pearl, Pascagoula, and Tombigbee. The most important lakes in Mississippi are man-made reservoirs, such as Pickwick Landing Reservoir on the Tennessee River. Other man-made lakes are Grenada Lake, and Arkabutla, Enid, and Sardis Reservoirs. One of the newest, the Ross Barnett Reservoir, is on the Pearl River near Jackson.

Below left:
Mississippi shrimp boats work the waters of the Gulf of Mexico. Trawls, which drag along the sea floor collecting shrimp, are suspended from the rigging of these boats. Mississippi supplies nearly a quarter of the shrimp canned annually in the United States.

Below right:
Cypress Swamp, near Jackson along the Natchez Trace, is characteristic of the heavily wooded, marshy land found in parts of southeastern Mississippi.

The *Delta Queen* and the *Mississippi Queen* are common sights in Natchez. Riverboats had a great impact on the development of mid-continent America, because they transported both cargo and passengers great distances and connected the traditions and cultures of people who lived along the banks of the river.

Summers are long and hot in Mississippi, with temperatures averaging 82 degrees Fahrenheit on the Gulf of Mexico and higher in the interior. However, cool breezes from the Gulf and frequent showers moderate the heat considerably. Snow is rare in the southern part of the state, but it does fall in the north, where winter temperatures average 48 degrees F. Mississippi lies in the paths of hurricanes traveling north from the Gulf and often experiences flooding and storm damage when these storms strike.

The History

Three powerful Indian tribes lived in the Mississippi region before white settlers arrived in the late seventeenth century. In the north and east were the Chickasaw, in the central area were the Choctaw, and in the southwest were the Natchez. These groups ruled the lesser tribes: the Chakchiuma, the Tunica, and the Yazoo, who lived along the Yazoo River, and the Biloxi and Pascagoula on the Gulf Coast. At the time of the earliest exploration by Europeans, there were between 25,000 and 30,000 Indians in the territory.

Eighty years before the *Mayflower* landed in Massachusetts, the Spanish explorer Hernando de Soto, coming west from his landing place in present-day Florida, became the first European to enter the Mississippi territory. He and his men discovered the Mississippi River. In 1682 the French explorer Robert Cavelier, who came down the Mississippi River from the Great Lakes to the Gulf of Mexico, claimed the whole Mississippi Valley in the name of King Louis XIV and named it Louisiana. This territory included what came to be the state of Mississippi.

Settlement began in 1699, when Pierre le Moyne established the French settlement at Old Biloxi, which is now known as Ocean Springs. Fort Rosalie, now Natchez, was founded in 1716 by Jean Baptiste le Moyne. Shortly thereafter, black slaves were brought in from Africa to work the rice and tobacco plantations established by the French.

John Law, a Scottish economist living in France, conceived a plan to develop the region in the early 1700s. Although it failed, like many schemes that underestimated the extent and the difficult conditions of the New World, Law's plan called attention to the possibilities of the new territory of Louisiana. At that time, Louisiana reached from the Allegheny Mountains to the Rockies, and French settlers began to emigrate into this vast frontier despite its hardships and dangers. The

Florewood Plantation, in Greenwood, was one of Mississippi's most prosperous cotton plantations before the Civil War.

Indians fought them to protect their ancestral lands. Then the British battled the French for possession of the territory. The French put down an uprising of the Natchez Indians in 1730, and in 1736 the Chickasaw, aided by the British, defeated the French in what is now northeastern Mississippi. The French had lost their chance to control the Mississippi Valley. The Chickasaw helped the British again in the French and Indian War (1754–63), in a blockade that prevented French troops in the lower Mississippi Valley from joining their comrades in the Ohio Valley to the north.

The Treaty of Paris, signed after the war, gave the British all the land east of the Mississippi River. The southern part of what is now Mississippi was annexed to the West Florida province, and the rest of the territory became part of the colony of Georgia.

West Florida remained loyal, for the most part, to the British Crown during the Revolutionary War (1775–83), but many Indians, trappers, and scouts in the rest of the Mississippi region supported the rebels. In 1781, the British, wearied by the war, let Spain take over

Above:
Stanton Hall is one of the stately mansions built in Natchez before the Civil War.

At left:
The grand homes of wealthy plantation owners in the South were decorated in a high style. Here, in the music parlor at Dunleith in Natchez, a "southern belle" re-creates the atmosphere of the middle 1800s.

West Florida. Fourteen years later, Spain agreed to accept most of the northern part of Mississippi as United States territory.

Congress established the Mississippi Territory in 1798, and in 1803, the Louisiana Purchase from France made the Mississippi River part of the United States. The access it provided to the Gulf of Mexico helped the territory to develop through trade. The Choctaw Indians under Chief Pushmataha were friendly to the Americans in Mississippi during the War of 1812 against Great Britain. They assisted General Andrew Jackson in fighting the Creek and defeating the British in the Battle of New Orleans.

The Mississippi Territory was divided by Congress in 1817 into the state of Mississippi and the Alabama Territory. That year, Mississippi became the 20th state of the Union. Columbia, Natchez, then Washington all served as state capitals until Jackson became the permanent capital in 1822. Ten years later most of the Indian tribes had given up and ceded their land to the United States. They moved to the Indian Territory that is now Oklahoma, and the lands they left were open to settlement. Settlers came from the East to farm, and found that most of the soil was ideal for cotton. In the early 1800s, Mississippi became one of the wealthiest states in the Union.

Most Mississippians were against secession, or withdrawal, from the Union in the years before the Civil War. But they strongly favored states' rights, especially regarding slavery, since their plantation economy depended on a cheap and plentiful labor supply. The state did secede in 1861, when the Civil War broke out. More than 80,000 troops from Mississippi served in the Confederate Army during the Civil War, and the state was the scene of many battles, including those at Vicksburg, Corinth, Harrisburg (which is now Tupelo), Holly Springs, Iuka, Jackson, Meridian, and Port Gibson. In June 1864, at Brice's Cross Roads, Cavalry General Nathan Bedford Forrest of Mississippi defeated a larger Union force. Reportedly, he attributed his success to the fact that he always tried "to git thar fustest with the mostest men." In any case, other generals of both North and South called Forrest the best cavalryman of the war.

Many Southerners were forced to live in these burrows in Vicksburg during the final days before the fall of the city in 1863. Vicksburg was the site of one of the Civil War's decisive battles. In order to facilitate Northern troop movements and to transport ammunition and other vital materials along the Mississippi River, the Union troops had to defeat a strong Southern fortification here. After the failure of an initial two-pronged attack by Union Generals Sherman and Grant, a string of brilliant strategical troop movements and attacks engineered by Grant finally forced Confederate Commander John C. Pemberton to surrender with his army of 30,000 men on July 4, 1863.

A photograph by Timothy Sullivan of General Ulysses S. Grant, who was elected President of the United States after the Civil War. Grant maneuvered his troops through the flooded bottomlands west of the Mississippi and masterminded the assault on Confederate troops at Vicksburg, where his victory made him one of the war's most famous heroes.

By far the most important of all the Mississippi battles was the one at Vicksburg, a key port on the Mississippi River. Union General Ulysses S. Grant and his troops took the city on July 4, 1863, after a 47-day siege whose climax coincided with the great battle at Gettysburg, Pennsylvania. This gave the Union control of the Mississippi River, and thus of the whole western part of the country, marking a vital turning point in the war. After Vicksburg and Gettysburg, the Confederate defeat was inevitable.

Mississippi was put under Union Army occupation during the bitter Reconstruction period that followed the war. It was not readmitted to the Union until 1870, after a new state constitution had been adopted. But at the turn of the new century, the state began to overcome the effects of the Civil War, and made rapid progress in agriculture, education, and industry. Lumbering became an important activity, and great swamp-drainage projects were begun. County agricultural high schools were set up, and an anti-illiteracy program was begun.

During World War I, which the United States entered in 1917, Payne Field was established at West Point, Mississippi, as an Army pilot training base. Camp Shelby, near Hattiesburg, was one of the most important training bases for American soldiers preparing for combat in Europe. The war ended the following year, and Mississippi made continued progress in agriculture until 1927, when a severe Mississippi River flood destroyed over $2 million worth of crops and property. This made people aware that agriculture should be balanced by industry, and during the Great Depression of the 1930s, Mississippi granted tax abatements and issued bonds to build new industry. When petroleum was discovered near Tinsley and at Vaughan in 1939–40, the economy took another upturn.

Many war plants operated in Mississippi during World War II (1941–45), and the port of Pascagoula became a shipbuilding center for convoy vessels, which accompanied battleships and supply ships on their wartime missions. The Atomic Energy Commission conducted nuclear experiments near Baxterville after the war, and the National Aeronautics and Space Administration tested rockets near Gulfport.

Today, Mississippi suffers from the 3rd highest unemployment rate in the country, it has the highest percentage (25%) of the population below the poverty line, and it has the lowest average income per family ($30,769) of any state. On the positive side, Mississippi has diversified its economy to include products such as: petroleum, forest products, natural gas, industrial clays, and food processing.

Commercial fishing is an important source of revenue, and state fisheries have recently turned to raising catfish—a traditional food

The beach at Biloxi, on the Gulf of Mexico, is one of the state's most popular resorts. It draws thousands of tourists annually and has helped Mississippi diversify its economy.

At right:
The musical traditions of Mississippi draw upon many different cultural backgrounds. Such popular forms as bluegrass and blues are rooted in the rural traditions of Southern whites and blacks. Here, a fiddler entertains a crowd at a country fair.

Below:
A Choctaw Indian woman in traditional dress. The Choctaw, Chickasaw, and Natchez were the three principal native tribes of what is now Mississippi. Though they were forced to give up most of their land over the years, a small community of Choctaw still lives near Philadelphia, in the east-central region of the state.

here, which is now in demand by other areas. Resort towns like Bay St. Louis, Biloxi, and Pass Christian, on the Gulf Coast, attract thousands of tourists annually.

Education

Legislation was passed establishing public schools in 1846. In 1862 the first schools for blacks were established creating a learning environment that was not completely segregated until 1970. Mississippi did not adhere to the 1954 U.S. Supreme Court decision outlawing racial segregation in public schools and many riots ensued, causing President John F. Kennedy to send Federal troops to Oxford, Mississippi. In 1968 the State University began accepting black students and in 1969 public elementary and secondary schools became integrated.

At left:
Novelist Richard Wright (1908–1960) was born near Natchez. During his career, Wright addressed forcefully the injustice of racism and illustrated through his characters the brutalizing effects of discrimination. His novel *Black Boy* was based on his early years in Mississippi. Wright's best-known work is *Native Son*, a bitter and poignant autobiography.

Below:
The study of Mississippi native novelist William Faulkner in Rowan Oak. He is perhaps best known for *The Sound and the Fury*, considered one of the greatest American novels. Faulkner was awarded the Nobel Prize for Literature in 1950 and received the Pulitzer Prize in 1955 and 1963.

The People

Just over 30 percent of Mississippians live in metropolitan areas. The majority of residents live in rural areas predominated by farms and small towns. Less than 99 percent of the residents were born in the United States. Mississippi has the third highest percentage (94%) of Christians in the U.S. Over half of the residents of the state are Baptists and about one-fourth are Methodists.

Famous People

Many famous people were born in the state of Mississippi. Here are a few:

Henry Armstrong 1912-1988, Columbus. Boxer who held featherweight, lightweight, and welterweight titles at the same time

Red Barber 1908-92, Columbus. Sports broadcaster

Theodore Bilbo 1877-1947, Juniper Grove. United States Senator for 12 years and Governor of Mississippi for 4 years who was accused of prohibiting blacks from voting

Craig Claiborne b.1920, Sunflower. Gourmet and food writer

Bo Diddley b.1928, McComb. Rock-and-roll singer

Charles Evers b.1922, Decatur. Civil rights leader

Medgar Evers 1925-1963, Decatur. Civil rights leader

William Faulkner 1897-1962, New Albany. Nobel Prize-winning novelist: *The Sound and The Fury, Absalom, Absalom!*

Bobbie Gentry b.1944, Chickasaw County. Country-and-western singer

Fanny Lou Hamer 1917-1977, Montgomery County. Civil rights leader

Jim Henson 1936-1990, Greenville. Creator of the Muppets

William Faulkner's writing was deeply rooted in the American South, but his themes were universal, insuring his popularity here and abroad.

James Earl Jones b.1931, Tate County. Award-winning stage and screen actor: *The Great White Hope, Field of Dreams*

B. B. King b.1925, Itta Bena. Rhythm-and-blues singer

John Avery Lomax 1867-1948, Goodman. Folk musicologist

Jimmie Lunceford 1902-1947, Fulton. Jazz band leader

Archie Manning b.1949, Drew. Football quarterback

Archie Moore b.1916, Benoit. Light-heavyweight boxing champion

Willie Morris b.1934, Jackson. Novelist and nonfiction writer: *North Toward Home, The Last of the Southern Girls*

Dave Parker b.1951, Calhoun. Baseball player

Elvis Presley 1935-1977, Tupelo. Rock-and-roll singer

Leontyne Price b.1927, Laurel. Operatic soprano

Charles Pride b.1939, Sledge.

Early on, Eudora Welty prepared for a career in advertising, but the success of her first short stories enabled her to pursue her love of writing full-time.

Country-and-western singer

Stella Stevens b. 1936, Yazoo City. Movie actress: *The Courtship of Eddie's Father, The Poseidon Adventure*

William Grant Still 1895-1978, Woodville. Composer, conductor

Ike Turner b.1939, Clarksdale. Pop singer

Conway Twitty 1933-93, Friar's Point. Country-and-western singer

Eudora Welty b.1909, Jackson. Pulitzer Prize-winning short-story writer and novelist: *The Optimist's Daughter*

Tennessee Williams 1911-1983, Columbus. Two-time Pulitzer Prize-winning dramatist: *A Streetcar Named Desire, Cat on a Hot Tin Roof*

Oprah Winfrey b.1954, Kosciusko. TV talk-show hostess

Richard Wright 1908-1960, near Natchez. Novelist: *Native Son, Black Boy*

Lester Young 1909-1959, Woodville. Jazz saxophonist

Colleges and Universities

There are many colleges and universities in Mississippi. Here are the more prominent, with their locations, dates of founding, and enrollments.

Alcorn State University, Lorman, 1871, 2,847.

Delta State University, Cleveland, 1924, 3,665.

Jackson State University, Jackson, 1877, 6,203.

Millsaps College, Jackson, 1890, 1,329.

Mississippi College, Clinton, 1826, 3,771.

Mississippi State University, Mississippi State, 1878, 14,619.

Mississippi University for Women, Columbus, 1884, 2,652.

Mississippi Valley State University, Itta Bena, 1946, 2,222.

University of Mississippi, University, 1844, 10,704.

University of Southern Mississippi, Hattiesburg, 1910, 11,680.

William Carey College, Hattiesburg, 1911, 2,032.

How to Get More Information

Mississippi Department of Economic Development & Community
P.O. Box 849
Jackson, Mississippi 39205-0849

94

Further Reading

General

Aylesworth, Thomas G., and Virginia L. *State Reports: Southern States.* New York: Chelsea House, 1991.

Alabama

Carpenter, Allan. *Alabama.* rev. ed. Chicago: Children's Press, 1978.

Fradin, Dennis B. *From Sea to Shining Sea: Alabama.* Chicago: Childrens Press, 1993.

Gray, Daniel S. *Alabama: A People, A Point of View.* Dubuque, Iowa: Kendall/Hunt, 1977.

Hamilton, Virginia B. *Alabama: A Bicentennial History.* New York: Norton, 1977.

Hamilton, Virginia B. *Alabama, A History.* New York: Norton, 1984.

McNair, Sylvia. *America the Beautiful: Alabama.* Chicago: Childrens Press, 1989.

Walker, Alyce B. ed. *Alabama: A Guide to the Deep South,* rev. ed. New York: Hastings House, 1975.

Florida

Carpenter, Allan. *Florida,* rev. ed. Chicago: Children's Press, 1979.

Fradin, Dennis B. *Florida in Words and Pictures.* Chicago: Children's Press, 1980.

Jahoda, Gloria. Florida: *A Bicentennial History.* New York: Norton, 1976.

Jahoda, Gloria. Florida: *A History.* New York: Norton, 1984.

Patrick, Rembert W., and A. C. Morris. *Florida Under Five Flags,* 4th ed. Gainesville, Florida: University Presses of Florida, 1967.

Smith, Mary Ellen. *Florida.* New York: Coward, 1970.

Stone, Lynn M. *America the Beautiful: Florida.* Chicago: Childrens Press, 1987.

Mississippi

Carpenter, Allan. *Mississippi,* rev. ed. Chicago: Children's Press, 1978.

Fraden, Dennis B. *Mississippi in Words and Pictures.* Chicago: Children's Press, 1980.

Larson, Robert. *America the Beautiful: Mississippi.* Chicago: Childrens Press, 1989.

Lowry, Robert, and W. H. McCardle. *A History of Mississippi.* Spartanburg, South Carolina: Reprint Company, 1978.

Newton, Carolyn S., and P. H. Coggin. *Meet Mississippi.* Huntsville, Alabama: Strode, 1976.

Rowland, Dunbar. *History of Mississippi, the Heart of the South.* 2 vols. Spartanburg, South Carolina: Reprint Company, 1978.

Sansing, David G. *Mississippi: Its People and Culture.* Minneapolis: Denison, 1981.

Skates, John Ray. *Mississippi: A Bicentennial History.* New York: Norton, 1979.

Skates, John R. *Mississippi, A History.* New York: Norton, 1985.

Numbers in italics refer to illustrations

Photo Credits

Courtesy of the Alabama State Archives: p. 30 (top); Courtesy of the Atlanta Braves: p. 30 (bottom); Courtesy of the Florida Department of Commerce/Division of Tourism: pp. 3 (bottom), 33, 34-35, 36-37, 38, 40, 42, 43, 44, 45, 46, 49, 50, 51, 52, 53, 54, 58, 61, 63; Courtesy of the Florida Department of State/Division of Library & Information Services: pp. 64, 65 (top); Courtesy of Robert Jordan: p. 76; Library of Congress: pp. 28, 57, 86-87; Courtesy of Merrill Lynch & Co., Inc.: p. 65 (bottom); Courtesy of the Miami Convention & Visitors Bureau: pp. 39, 47, 48; Courtesy of the Mississippi Department of Economics & Community Development: p. 67; Courtesy of the Mississippi Office of Travel and Tourism: pp. 4, 68-69, 70-71, 73, 74, 75, 77, 78, 79, 80, 81, 83, 84, 89, 90, 91 (bottom), 93; National Portrait Gallery, Smithsonian Institution: pp. 25 (left), 29, 59, 88, 91 (top); Courtesy of the State of Alabama Bureau of Tourism & Travel: pp. 3, 5, 6-7, 8-9, 13, 14, 15, 16-17, 18-19, 20, 21, 23, 24, 25 (right), 26, 27; Courtesy of the State of Mississippi/Department of Archives & History: p. 92; Stokes Collection, New York Public Library: pp. 56, 60.
Cover photographs courtesy of the Florida Department of Commerce/Division of Tourism; the Mississippi Office of Travel and Tourism; and the State of Alabama Bureau of Tourism & Travel.